## Justine versus the baby . . .

Cassidy stood by the window, pushing all of the baby's things out and squealing with delight as they fell to the patio below. I imagined Mrs. Holmes coming home to find splattered toys and baby powder and rattles lying all over the backyard.

I closed the door to the baby's room and sprinted down the stairs. Outside, I gathered up everything as quickly as I could, blew away the spilled powder, and headed back to the house. I reached to push open the back door. It didn't move.

I put down the toys and tried to turn the handle. Nothing. Shielding my eyes from the sun, I peeked through the glass door. There was Cassidy, a triumphant grin on her face. The little brat had locked me out!

# Justine's Baby-Sitting Nightmare

# The Boyfriend Club

# Justine's Baby-Sitting Nightmare

## Janet Quin-Harkin

**Rainbow Bridge®**
**Troll Associates**

*For Penny, Jane, and Linda, who made up the foursome of my youth and whose friendship has survived the test of years and miles.*

# 1

"You know the best thing about not having a boy-friend?" Karen asked.

It was a warm Saturday night in May, and the four of us were lying in our sleeping bags on Roni's patio, watching the stars. We all jumped up at the mention of boyfriends.

"Being able to flirt with every cute guy in the class?" Ginger said immediately. She's been going with the same guy for almost the whole school year. I guess she misses flirting.

"Knowing that you're a free and liberated woman, not tied to some guy who will never understand the essence of your personality?" Roni suggested. She's the dramatic one—she just had one of the leads in our last play. Obviously, she's dramatic offstage too.

It was clearly my responsibility to come up with the correct answer to Karen's question.

"Not having to worry about wearing clothes he likes?" I suggested. "Although *your* boyfriend was not what anyone would call a fashion expert, Karen." Her ex-boyfriend had worn capes and suspenders. Enough said.

"As if I have much choice in what I wear, Justine," Karen said. "You know my wardrobe: one pair of jeans and some pleated skirts. I'm stuck looking the same no matter what guy I go out with." Karen comes from a very strict, old-fashioned family. If her mother had her way, Karen would still wear a uniform like she did at parochial school.

Karen sat up and hugged her knees. "No, what I was really thinking is that it's great to be able to get together with you guys on a Saturday night without any hassle. James always sulked if I didn't want to spend time with him."

"And his computer," Roni added.

Karen nodded. "That's another thing. It's great to be able to do things that I like too."

"I know," Roni said. "That's one of the reasons

I'm not planning to get too serious with Drew again. I know we like each other, but I just can't afford to do the things he does. Besides, I don't particularly want to spend every weekend horseback riding or skydiving. I'm happier hanging out with you guys, going to the mall, and then sleeping over at someone's house."

"At least that shows she has good taste," I said to the others. "Anyone who prefers my company to Drew Howard's—"

"Needs their head examined," Karen said quickly. "Just kidding, Justine," she added hastily. "But you have to admit that Drew is the cutest guy you're ever likely to meet."

"I do not have to admit that," I said. "I plan to meet a guy who's even cuter than Drew . . . someday."

"Dream on, Justine." Ginger chuckled.

"It's possible," I said. "Drew's not the only cute guy in the universe, you know, and I am blossoming to the peak of my natural beauty." I waited while they stopped choking and rolling around before I went on.

"I know my perfect guy is out there somewhere, and he's everything I've been waiting for—he'll drive a Porsche, he'll be an incredible dancer, an athlete, intelligent, sensitive . . . oh, and rich, of course."

I shrugged as the others laughed. "There's someone out there like that. I know it," I said. "And what's more, I'm going to find him."

"What about Danny?" Ginger asked, lying back on her pillow again.

"What about him?" I asked cautiously.

"Are you planning to dump him when you find this dream guy?"

I gave a nervous little laugh. "Danny's just a high school sweetheart, nothing serious. You don't think I'm going to date him forever, do you? I'm surprised we've been together this long! We have nothing in common."

"So you think it's time for a change?" Karen asked. I saw her exchange glances with Ginger, and a cold shiver went up my spine. It was an innocent enough question, but it made me wonder. Had they come to the same conclusion as I had about what we'd seen in the cafeteria last week?

We didn't usually eat in the cafeteria, but a sudden spring storm had soaked the ground under our favorite tree, so we'd gone to join the chaos inside. Just as we came through the door, a girl had run toward us, squealing, while some guy tried to put an ice cube down her back.

"I'll get you back, Michelle Greiner," he was yelling. But he was laughing and so was she. The whole thing seemed pretty normal . . . except for one little thing. The guy was Danny. It took a second to register that it was *my* boyfriend flirting like this.

It was no big deal, really. I mean, Danny's free to put ice cubes down anyone's back if he wants. But the fact that it happened to be Michelle Greiner, who I have to admit is gorgeous (even if she is a stuck-up snob), made me feel very insecure. I kept telling myself that Danny was only being his usual teasing self. But you don't put ice cubes down just anyone's back, do you? You only do that to someone you sort of like. And that was a scary thought. Danny and I had broken up before, and it was terrible. We'd made up that time, but now I was afraid all over again.

It wasn't as if Danny was the big love of my life or anything. I mean, I wouldn't die of a broken heart if we split up for good. But we'd been together for so long. He was fun to be around, even if we were totally different. I couldn't imagine being without him.

But I wasn't about to be dumped, especially not for Michelle Greiner. If anyone was going to do the dumping, it was Justine Craft!

13

I took a deep breath and lay back on the warm stone of Roni's patio, staring at the stars again. "Maybe it is time for a change," I said, trying to keep my voice light. "I think it's a big mistake being tied down to one guy when you're only a freshman in high school. I bet that's why so many people get divorced—they don't get enough dating experience first. My mother started going with my father when she was only seventeen, and look what happened to *them*."

Oops. I'd meant to keep the conversation light and now look what I'd brought up—just about the heaviest thing I could think of! My mom had walked out on Dad and me when I was just a little kid, and I hadn't seen her since. Truthfully, I was so young that I don't remember much about her. But there's still a big empty hole in my middle when I watch other kids with their mothers.

My dad kept telling me that I had Christine now. And I did, whether I wanted her or not! I couldn't think of Christine as a mother, no matter how hard I tried. For one thing, she was way too young. For another, she didn't have time to be *my* mother. All she and Dad could think about was the baby they were expecting any day now.

"Justine's right," Karen said. "We need to play the field, find out what's out there. . . ."

14

"And then latch onto the guy with the longest eyelashes," Roni quipped.

"And the gold Porsche," I finished for her. "That will be my next assignment for the Boyfriend Club—long eyelashes and a gold Porsche. And a sense of humor. And maybe a math whiz, so he can do my homework for me."

"You don't want much, do you?" Ginger said, throwing her pillow at me. The others joined in with pillows and rude comments. It was hard to stay depressed for long when I was around my friends. Whenever we were together, good things happened . . . like forming a club to find ourselves boyfriends. It's never worked, of course. But it's fun anyway.

We were in the middle of a real pillow battle when we noticed a little figure standing in the doorway, like a small white ghost.

"Roni," the figure whimpered. It was Roni's little brother, Paco, looking incredibly cute in his tiny flannel pj's. Roni's parents were out for the evening and we had been left in charge of the kids.

Instantly Roni jumped up and ran over to him. Questions and answers in Spanish followed. Although I've taken Spanish for two years now, and

15

I've actually been to Spain, it was too quick for me to follow.

Then Roni scooped him up into her arms. "He had a bad dream," she explained. "I'm going to make him some hot chocolate and put him back to bed."

We followed her inside. Ginger held Paco while Roni put on the water for the chocolate.

"What was your bad dream about?" Ginger asked him.

"Monsters! Big ugly ones," he said in perfect English. He understands much more than his family thinks he does.

When the chocolate was ready, Roni carried Paco to his bedroom and I followed with the steaming cup. She sat with him while he sipped the hot chocolate, then tucked him into bed and sang some little songs to him. Paco's face became sleepy. He put his thumb in his mouth, and soon he was asleep.

The rest of us watched from the doorway. Ginger and Karen kept whispering about how cute he was and how much fun it would be to have a little brother. But my insides were doing flip-flops. In a couple of weeks, I'd be a big sister too. And I had just realized that I didn't know a thing about babies! How did Roni know that hot chocolate would work? How did she know what songs to sing? How did she know how to carry Paco without dropping him or hurting him?

"No more monsters," Roni said, giving us a grin as she ushered us out of Paco's room. "Do you guys want some hot chocolate?"

"Are you going to tuck us in and sing us lullabies, Mama Roni?" Ginger teased.

"Shut up." Roni gave her a friendly shove. Those two have known each other since they were five years old, and they're always teasing.

"I thought you did it very well," said Karen, who's always the peacemaker. "I was impressed."

"So was I," I said. "I don't know anything about babies."

"All you have to know is which end to diaper and which end to feed," Roni said.

"Diaper?" I wrinkled my nose. "Are you crazy? I don't do diapers, thank you. I don't mind singing a lullaby or two, but nothing messy."

"Babies are messy all the time, Justine," Roni said. "You just have to get used to it."

"I don't think I'll ever want to get used to it," I said.

"But Justine," Ginger said. "You'll have to do

diapers if you want to help take care of your little brother or sister."

"I can't imagine Christine changing diapers either," I said. "Her perfect fingernails would probably claw the baby to pieces! Besides, she hates getting her clothes dirty."

"Is she planning to hire a nanny, then?" Karen asked.

"I don't know. They're still talking about it," I said. "In fact, that's all they talk about these days. Baby this, baby that—it's nauseating. I guess I shouldn't worry, though, because they're not going to let me anywhere near the baby."

"Sure they will, Justine," Roni said. "My mom was always happy when I helped her. I used to love giving the little ones their baths. I got to play with their tub toys even though I was too old!"

"Yeah, well, your family isn't exactly like mine," I said. "And they're your real sisters and brother, not just half siblings. I get the feeling that the family at my house will consist of my dad, Christine, and the baby. I'll just be someone who lives there. Whenever they pass me on the stairs they'll say, 'Oh, are you still here?'"

My friends laughed and shook their heads. "Come on, Justine. It won't be like that and you know it," Roni said. "Christine will welcome your help when the baby arrives. You told us yourself that she's been trying very hard to be friends with you."

"Until recently," I said. "When she had nothing better to do. But now that the baby's almost here, it's all she can think about. Every day she comes home with another pile of baby clothes or a cute little bunny or something. I tell you, that kid is in serious danger of being buried under a mountain of stuffed animals. And when Dad comes home at night, all they do is study books of names. They won't let me anywhere near the baby because they'll be terrified I'll do something wrong—and they're probably right!"

"Then you should get some practice before the baby arrives," Karen suggested.

"What do you mean, practice dressing my dolls?"

"No." Karen laughed. "I mean with real babies."

"Like baby-sitting, you mean?"

"Sure," Roni said. "That's a great idea. I've grown up as an unpaid baby-sitter, and Ginger baby-sits for money. So we've gotten our experience that way."

"That's one of the disadvantages of being rich, I guess," I said. "I never needed to baby-sit."

"One of the disadvantages?" Karen spluttered. "Tell me the others! I'd sure take them over the disadvantages of being poor."

"No, you wouldn't," I said seriously. "Getting sent away to boarding schools and summer camps is no fun. I thought I'd hate it at a big public high school, but I've never had friends like you guys before. I sure hope Dad and Christine don't put my little brother or sister through the same thing."

"Then you have to stop them, Justine," Karen said. "If you're a real help to Christine in bringing up this baby, then you'll have a say in how its life turns out."

"And the baby will look up to you," Roni said. "I just love it when Paco wraps his arms around my neck and gives me kisses. There's no feeling like it."

A picture was forming in my mind . . . my little sister, dressed in a mini designer outfit just like mine, holding my hand while I showed her the mall. "This is the kind of store we shop in," I'd tell her, "and this is how you use a charge card." And everyone would stare at us and whisper, "Aren't they adorable?"

Maybe it wouldn't be so bad after all. If I could just figure out how babies worked, then maybe I would have fun being a big sister! And maybe, just maybe, I'd have someone who thought I was special and loved me best.

# Chapter

## 2

As Karen's dad drove me home the next morning, I was full of big plans. I'd get some baby-sitting experience and then I'd surprise Dad and Christine with my expert handling of the kid. Driving home across deserted Sunday morning Phoenix to our more upscale area near Scottsdale, I let myself drift into a daydream:

*The baby was crying and crying. Nobody could stop it. Then I waltzed in (wearing a great outfit by Donna Karan!) and said sweetly, "Let me try." The baby immediately stopped crying and smiled up at me adoringly. Dad and Christine looked at me with admiration and whispered that I had a wonderful way with babies and they were so glad I was around.*

All I had to do was find a kid to practice on. It shouldn't be too hard—people were always desperate for baby-sitters, right? I'd just look in the classified ads in the Sunday paper, pick the best one, and cram in a few weeks of baby-sitting practice.

As I put my key in the door, it occurred to me that I knew zero, zilch, *nada* about babies. I wondered if that would be a problem. Parents can be picky when it comes to their darling kids.

I could hear the sound of voices coming from the master bedroom. Dad and Christine were having their usual leisurely Sunday breakfast in bed with the newspapers—or maybe it was with the baby books. I crept past and went into my room.

I have a big walk-in closet with a ton of stuff crammed into it, so it took a while to look through everything. But finally I found the toy chest with my old dolls in it. I laid them all out on my bed and picked one that was about the size of a real baby. I'd never really been into dolls, except for Barbies—I could dress those in designer outfits. I couldn't remember ever playing house or pretending to be a mommy. Maybe that was because I didn't remember having a mommy around.

I picked up the doll by the arm, before I remembered that it was supposed to be a real baby. I didn't think babies liked to be carried around that way! So I held it underneath its body and carried it to the nursery. The room was completely ready for the new baby and it looked perfect. In fact, it looked like a baby's room from a movie set. The crib had white lace frills around it and a handmade pastel quilt. There was a mobile above it and adorable wallpaper with ducks.

I tiptoed in and pulled back the quilt. It wasn't easy, because I was still holding the doll. How did mothers have enough hands? Anyway, I managed to put the doll under the quilt. Then I tucked it in.

"Sleep tight; don't let the bedbugs bite," I said. That's what my dad used to say to me. Then I remembered that Roni had sung to her brother to put him to sleep. I tried to remember one of those baby songs, but I couldn't get past the first line of "Twinkle, Twinkle, Little Star." So I hummed some of the rock songs I knew instead.

I was so into this that I didn't hear the door open behind me. All of a sudden I heard a shriek. "Justine, what are you doing?" Christine yelled.

Of course, that brought my father running. "What is it? What's happening?" he cried. "Justine, what have you done?"

"Nothing," I said angrily. "Chill out, for pete's sake."

"It's okay," Christine said, putting her hand to her throat and gasping dramatically. Even Roni wouldn't have hammed it up that much. "I was just surprised to see her in here. I can wash the sheets and everything—that doll doesn't look *too* dirty."

My father put an arm around her. "It's okay, punkin," he soothed. Then he glared at me. "This isn't your playroom, Justine," he said coldly. "Aren't you a little old for dolls? We don't want your toys getting germs all over the baby's things."

I felt as if I was a bubble and somebody had popped me. No, it was worse than that. I felt as if someone had punched me in the stomach and taken my breath away. "Toys!" I snapped. "That's the last time I try and do anything nice for you guys! Just forget it. In fact, forget I even exist."

I pushed past them both and ran to my room, slamming the door behind me. I could hardly catch my breath, and I definitely couldn't calm down. Everything wasn't going to be okay after all. It was Christine and the precious baby who mattered. I was just someone who was in the way, someone they didn't want anywhere near them.

I felt tears stinging my eyes and I fought them down. I hate to cry. I wasn't going to cry. Well, if that's what they wanted, I'd stay out of their way.

Just wait until they wanted to go out and they needed a baby-sitter. Then I'd remind them that they told me to stay away from the baby's room, that I wasn't welcome there. And there was no way I'd bother with a stupid baby-sitting job. I'd find other things to do with my life—fun things.

There was a tap on my door. I didn't answer. Then my father's voice said softly, "Justine? Can I come in, please?" He didn't wait for an answer, but opened the door. "Can we talk for a minute?" he asked.

"What for?" I demanded. "Are you going to tell me what parts of the house I'm allowed in? Are you moving my bedroom down to the cellar so I don't contaminate the baby?"

He laughed and ruffled my hair. I turned away angrily.

"I'm sorry if I yelled, princess," he said. "It's just that Christine shouldn't be upset right now. You know how hard she worked to make the baby's room perfect."

"Does anyone ever think that I shouldn't be upset right now?" I said, staring out the window. "I have feelings too, you know."

"I know that, sweetheart. I'm sure you didn't mean any harm. Christine reminded me that you

25

didn't have much of a childhood, shipped from one school to the next. I guess you never had a chance to play with dolls like other girls."

I turned around and eyed him coldly. "For your information, I was not playing with dolls," I said. "I've never been around babies before, so I was trying to get the feel of it with a doll, before I had to touch the real thing. I wanted to know what I was doing so I could help after the baby is born. I didn't expect Christine to get so upset over a stupid doll."

"Practicing with a doll, huh?" he said with a grin. "Good thinking, Justine. Good idea. Smart kid." Then he ruffled my hair again and left the room, still chuckling. I noticed that he hadn't apologized.

All day they tried extra hard to be nice to me. Christine found a bunch of books for me to read on baby care and baby psychology. There was even one called *The Miracle of Birth*, which had disgusting pictures in it. I decided on the spot that if I wanted kids someday, I'd adopt. But no matter how hard they tried, they couldn't undo what they'd already done. I couldn't shake off the hollow feeling that I was an outsider in my own family. When it came down to the nitty-gritty, I was only in the way.

*Let them give me every dumb book in the world,* I told myself. *They're not going to win me over. If they don't want me anywhere near their precious darling, then fine. I'll stay away. I'll stay away from all of them.*

I'd put the idea of baby-sitting out of my mind, so I was startled when Karen greeted me the next morning by saying, "Justine, guess what? I've found the perfect job for you."

"Job? What kind of job?" Modeling, professional tennis player, star ballerina . . . all these things flashed through my mind before Karen said, "Baby-sitting. What else?"

"Oh, that," I said. "Thanks, but no thanks."

"But, Justine, we talked about it over the weekend. We agreed that you needed to practice before the baby arrives."

"Not anymore," I said, and I told her what had happened on Sunday morning.

As usual, Karen immediately saw their point of view. "It's not so bad, Justine. You just surprised Christine, that's all. She probably doesn't care that much about the doll getting the crib dirty."

"Then why did they yell at me?" I demanded. "They obviously don't want me around. Don't take their side."

She turned away. "Sorry. I was only trying to

help. I didn't mean to upset you," she said.

Then she went on calmly loading books into her locker. They were all stacked neatly—unlike in my locker, where everything falls out every time I open it. I jammed my books into my locker, feeling bad. Karen is just about the sweetest person around. I knew she really was trying to make me feel better and that I'd upset her. After a while I couldn't stand it any longer.

"Look, I'm sorry if I yelled," I said, "but you don't understand what it's like. Every time I think things are going okay at home, something happens to make me feel like I don't belong there, like I don't matter. Yesterday was the last straw. I know they don't want to risk me anywhere near their precious child."

"I'm sure that's not true, Justine," Karen said. "You've got to stop being jealous of this baby."

"Jealous? Who said anything about being jealous?" I demanded.

Karen just shrugged, took some books from her locker, and stuffed them into her backpack. The bell rang.

I followed Karen to class, feeling miserable. The last thing I wanted now was a fight with my friends. They were all I had.

# Chapter 3

The day hadn't started out too well, and it sure didn't get much better. We had a surprise pop quiz in English—the kind of dumb quiz I hate, when the teacher actually expects you to have read the book and asks questions like what color some character's hat was. As if that matters.

Then, after English, as I was crossing the main quad to get back to my locker, I happened to glance into the shadows along the gym wall. I saw Danny with Michelle. They weren't doing anything except talking, but Michelle had her back against the wall and Danny was facing her. He was leaning over her with one hand propped on the wall close to her face—the sort of position a guy would take when he wants to kiss a girl but hasn't gotten up the courage yet. As I looked at them, I knew that I hadn't imagined it. There was something going on between Danny and Michelle.

My first instinct was to go right up to them and make a big scene. I wanted to grab Michelle and accuse her of being a boyfriend stealer. Then I wanted to push her into the nearest puddle. Unfortunately it hadn't rained for a week now and the hot sun had long ago dried any puddles.

*If only I were still at Sagebrush Academy*, I thought. My old school was way up in the mountains, where there were plenty of cliffs I could have pushed Michelle over. Maybe Danny too, for being so sneaky.

That was what I hated most. It hurt me to think that my boyfriend was sneaking around with another girl without telling me. It would have been so much easier to handle if he'd come right out and told me that he wanted to break up. Sure, I'd still be upset, but I'd have gotten over it. This way, I was angry and scared at the same time.

I wasn't only scared about losing Danny. I was scared that other people would see him with Michelle and feel sorry for me. Having people pity me is something I just can't handle. I'm used to being the kind of person other people envy. Justine has it all, that's what they usually say. She's rich, she's talented, she's great-looking. How could I face anybody at school if they looked at me with pity?

I pretended I hadn't seen anything. Instead, I hurried on to my next class. If that was the way Danny was going to behave, I was better off without him. It was time for a change anyway. It was stupid to date one person for so long at our age. I should be experiencing Life with a capital *L*, flirting, having fun, meeting new guys all the time. No commitments, no relationships that got too serious. Maybe I'd even start a Guy of the Week Club and work my way through all the cute guys at Alta Mesa. The whole world was mine now that I was free from Danny.

I kept telling myself this over and over, all through my next class, which happened to be Spanish. I even practiced the bright, perky smile I'd wear when Danny officially told me the news.

"Do you have a joke you'd like to share with the rest of us, Justine?" Señora Rojas asked, making me realize that I'd better stop practicing the smile until school was out.

I just hoped I wouldn't bump into Danny and Michelle while I was with my friends at lunch.

They wouldn't be sure that I knew, so they'd try not to talk about Danny. They'd try to spare my feelings, and I hate that. I practically dragged them along the path to our favorite tree.

"Hey, what's the big rush?" Ginger demanded. "Slow down, Justine. We don't have to sprint to lunch."

"I just want to make sure nobody else has taken our tree," I lied. "I heard some kids talking about eating outside. They might pick our tree if we don't get there fast."

"So we find another tree," Karen said easily. "We don't have to eat lunch in the same place for the rest of our lives, you know."

"But I like that tree," I said, knowing that I sounded pretty lame. "It has a special meaning for me. It has history."

Roni looked at Ginger and grinned. "Is this the same girl who throws out her entire wardrobe every six months because it's out of date?"

"Clothes are different," I said. "Clothes go out of style. Trees don't."

"Very deep, Justine," Karen said, laughing. "Maybe you should sign up for philosophy next year."

"Uh . . . no, thanks," I said quickly. "They don't do Cliffs Notes for all those old Greek guys."

We raced around the last corner and there was our tree, shady, majestic . . . and unoccupied. I let out a sigh of relief. It was like coming home. We threw down our lunch bags and were arranging ourselves on the ground when I heard a high, maniacal laugh.

I knew that laugh. It belonged to Owen, Lord of the Nerds. Instantly we grabbed our things again, ready for flight. Being trapped by nerds while we were trying to eat was not an experience we liked to have. I snuck a glance in their direction. There were only four of them today, only the hard-core nerds, but that was bad enough. Owen was the shortest guy in the freshman class. I bet he was the shortest fourteen-year-old in the entire country. And the most repulsive one. Why the others obeyed him, we've never figured out. Any one of them could have squished him with his little finger. Wolfgang, the roly-poly nerd, could have squashed him flat without noticing.

My friends always tried to be nice to them because they felt sorry for them. Roni had even dated one of the fringe nerds, but that was now over, thank goodness. I didn't see why we had to be nice to them. They were flat-out annoying.

The nerd pack was only a few feet from us, and

it seemed that flight was impossible. So we braced ourselves and waited for the nerd attack. But the nerds actually started to pass without talking to us. It was a miracle!

"Look, there's Justine," I heard Owen say. "Don't let her know that you've seen her."

"But don't you think we should tell her—" Ronald began.

"Shhh! Do you want her to hear you?" Owen warned.

"But I think she should know," Ronald insisted.

I couldn't stand it any longer. It simply wasn't possible that even the nerds knew about Danny and me breaking up. If they did, the news really must be all over school. "Tell me what?" I yelled.

"Nothing. Nothing at all," Owen said instantly. "It was another Justine we were talking about. Enjoy your lunch."

"Tell me what, Ronald?" I insisted.

Ronald blushed. "About what we saw and we thought you should know, because it concerns you, but we weren't sure how to break it to you. . . ."

"I said to shut up, Ronald. It's none of our business," Owen said.

"That's right, Ronald," Wolfgang chimed in with his big, deep voice. "Owen's right. It would only hurt her feelings if she knew that her boyfriend was sitting in the cafeteria with another girl on his lap."

"You jerk, Wolfgang," Owen said, hitting him with his briefcase. "What did I tell you? Don't ever speak unless you check with me first."

"Sorry, Owen. It just sort of slipped out," Wolfgang said.

If I hadn't been so horrified, it would have been like watching an old Laurel and Hardy movie. I couldn't stand another second of seeing pity in nerdy eyes.

"Oh, that's okay, guys," I said. "Danny and I are history. Who he flirts with now is none of my business. But thanks for thinking of me. Now, if you'll excuse us, we're just about to eat lunch and I find it hard to digest food when you're around."

"Sure, okay, no problem," they muttered as they started to move away again.

I sat down and tore the wrapper off my sandwich. It was shrimp and avocado, but it tasted like sawdust. I made myself chew it, but for some reason, I couldn't swallow it.

"Did you really already know about Danny and Michelle?" Ginger asked cautiously. "Did you and Danny really break up?"

"I knew," I said breezily. "What did I tell you

guys on Saturday? I said I was getting bored, right? So this suits me just fine. Now we can both move on. It doesn't bother me at all."

"That's good to know, Justine," Karen said gently. "We wouldn't want to see you get hurt. I'm sure Michelle Greiner is just someone he likes to flirt with. Danny hates phonies."

I shrugged. "Who he dates is up to him," I said. "Obviously he's going for a complete opposite to try and get me out of his system. He had a girlfriend with taste and style, and now he's got one with a laugh that sounds like a barnyard animal."

The others grinned.

"I'm glad you're taking this so well, Justine," Roni said. "It's not easy when a long relationship breaks up, I know. So if you're ever feeling down and you need to talk, remember we're always here and we're on your side."

"Thanks, but I'm going to be just fine," I said. "In fact, I'm really excited. Now there's nothing in the way of meeting that guy with the Porsche. Danny can't even drive yet. I'm planning to move up the evolutionary ladder."

I was almost beginning to believe myself. I found myself checking out upperclassmen as I walked through the halls that afternoon. I wasn't sure how I was actually going to meet one, but that didn't matter. I'd get the Boyfriend Club to figure it out. After all, I was one of the most mature freshpersons around, and I did have the best fashion sense of anyone in my class, as well as my classic Nordic beauty, so it shouldn't be too hard. All I had to do was pick my Guy of the Week and get moving.

I was impressed with myself. It just showed how mature and cool I had become this year. When I saw Danny, I knew exactly what I'd say to him. I'd even be classy enough not to mention Michelle.

And then, as we were getting out of math class, Danny came up behind me and grabbed my arm.

"Justine, I need to talk to you. Have you got a minute?"

The feel of his hand on my arm sent that old electricity racing through me. I was so aware of his closeness, of those deep brown eyes and that cute little dimple in his chin when he smiled. I tried to remember all the cool things I was going to say to him, but my mind went blank.

"Oh, uh . . . sure," I stammered. *Get it together, Justine,* I ordered myself. *Act cool, just like you've been practicing all day. Don't let him see that he's got you rattled!* I made a supreme effort and smiled the perky smile from Spanish class.

"What's on your mind, Danny?" Yeah, that was great. That sounded really cool. "I really only have a minute," I went on breathlessly, "because I have to dash."

"Why?"

I tried to think of something fun and impressive that I was really late for, but for some reason all I could come up with was, "My new job."

"What job? Since when did you get a job?"

"Baby-sitting." It just came out.

A big grin spread across Danny's face. "You? Someone actually let you loose with a baby?"

"Why not?" I demanded. It was easier to act superior now that he was annoying me. "Why should I be different from any other girl?"

His grin spread even wider. "Oh, come on, Jus. Since when do you need extra money? Or did your credit card fall down a drain?"

"For your information," I said, really cool now, "this has nothing to do with money. I decided to become an expert on babies before my little sister or brother arrives. So I've got this terrific baby-sitting job, every evening after school and weekends too. I was meaning to talk to you about it, but I've been so busy . . . I just hope you understand that I don't really have time for you right now. I mean, time for us right now."

"You don't?" That clearly threw him for a curve.

I was on a roll now, hardly aware of what I was babbling about. "No, I don't. Not with the baby-sitting and then the new baby coming any day. So I hope you won't take it too hard if I suggest that we should maybe break up, at least for a while."

"Break up? You're breaking up with me?" He was still looking dazed, as if he couldn't believe what he was hearing.

I smiled sympathetically. "Let's face it, Danny. It's kind of dumb to get too serious at our age. You'll always be special to me and all, but it really is time to move on, don't you think? We should both be seeing other people. You do agree, don't you?"

He blinked. He swallowed. "Uh, yeah, great idea, Justine. I'd been feeling pretty much the same way."

"Good! Then we can both get on with our lives with no hard feelings."

He had a silly grin on his face now. "Uh . . . right. No hard feelings. You don't know how glad I am that we've had this talk. I feel so much better now. Thanks a million, Justine." He squeezed my arm. "Well, I better let you get to your baby-sitting job. See you around."

Then he leaned across and gave me a peck on

my cheek. I really wished he hadn't done that. Until that moment I'd been just fine. But the warmth of his lips on my cheek reminded me—this was Danny, the first special guy in my life.

And now he'd never kiss me again.

# Chapter

## 4

I was fine until I got home. It was only as I let myself into that big, empty house and stood in the hallway listening to the deep ticking of the grandfather clock that it finally hit me. *It's all over. No more Danny, ever.*

I fought back the urge to throw a temper tantrum. I reminded myself of all the good things that could happen now. I even went into the kitchen and got myself a huge bowl of pistachio ice cream with chocolate syrup, but the hurt wouldn't go away. And the hurt was so strong it surprised me—I'd been so worried about my pride that I hadn't thought about my heart. I couldn't even swallow the ice cream.

I knew that it was probably a good thing we'd broken up, and that I shouldn't be serious with one guy at my age, but it didn't make me feel any better. I missed Danny already. I didn't know what I was going to do without him. How could I stand seeing him with Michelle Greiner? Watching him hold her hand in school?

I picked up the phone a couple of times to call my friends, but I always put it down again. I'd told them that I wanted out, that I was glad we broke up. So I couldn't call them now and tell them how awful I really felt. It would be great to hear Karen's soft gentle voice, or Roni's laugh, but my stupid pride wouldn't let me call.

I lay back on my bed and hugged my big stuffed gorilla. He was soft and squishy and I clung to him fiercely. I felt so empty inside, I wouldn't have been surprised if you could see right through me. I didn't matter to anyone in the whole world anymore. My dad had Christine and they'd both have the baby. And now Danny had a new girlfriend. I had nobody.

But I would never let them know they had gotten to me, I decided, hugging my gorilla so hard that my hands almost met. Nobody would know. They'd all see me looking as perfect and happy as ever and they'd never know what was going on in-side. Roni wasn't the only actress around here.

All I had to do was keep busy enough so that I didn't have time to think. Suddenly baby-sitting didn't seem like such a bad idea. It couldn't hurt if I knew more about babies than Christine did, and it would keep me totally occupied. Maybe I'd even find an adorable little kid who'd fling his arms around me the way Roni's brother hugged her.

I let go of my gorilla. "You're no good. You don't know how to hug back," I said. "I'm going to find a real live kid who thinks I'm the greatest thing since cellular phones."

The next morning I grabbed Karen as soon as she came into school.

"That baby-sitting job you told me about—I want it after all. Where is it? How old is the baby? When can I start?"

"Gee, Justine," Karen said, looking embarrassed. "When you said you weren't interested, I asked my neighbor if she'd like to do it."

"But I really want that job, Karen. Can't you tell her you made a mistake?"

"I can't do that, Justine. She needs the money. She was so excited to get it."

43

"But what about me?" I demanded. "I really need it too. How about I pay her not to take it?"

Karen rolled her eyes. "There are other jobs, Justine. If you really want a baby-sitting job, I'm sure you'll find one with no problem."

"But how? Where?"

"Neighbors. Friends of your parents."

"My neighbors usually have live-in nannies from Europe," I said. "And my parents' friends are the same."

"Well, ask around at school," Karen suggested. "Maybe you can find someone with more baby-sitting jobs than they can handle."

That seemed like a good idea, until I remembered that I'd told Danny I already had a job. If he found out I was still looking, he'd realize I had been lying about wanting to break up. I shook my head firmly. "I don't want people at school to know that I'm looking for a baby-sitting job. It's bad for my image."

Karen stared at me like I was nuts. "Then I suppose you have to look in the want ads," she said. "I've never tried it myself, but there must be people looking for child care."

"That's a good idea," I said. "That way I can go check out the family first and make sure they're my kind of people. I wouldn't want to be stuck with a kid who's not right for me."

Karen just shook her head and laughed.

At lunchtime I snuck out of school, even though freshmen weren't allowed off campus, and bought a newspaper from the 7-Eleven. Then I hurried back to my friends under the tree.

"Okay," I said, flinging the paper down and narrowly missing Ginger's tuna sandwich. "Get busy. You have to help me find the perfect child to baby-sit."

"How will you know if it's the perfect child, Justine?" Ginger asked.

"That's easy," Roni replied. "The ad will say 'Adorable two-year-old, into designer baby clothes, already has own drool-proof credit card.'"

"And pedal Porsche," Karen added.

"Pedal? Are you crazy?" Ginger sniffed. "That is so common. You mean electric Porsche."

"Solar-powered Porsche?" Roni suggested. "They're environmentally correct, remember."

"Shut up, you guys," I said, laughing with them. "I've never done this before! How am I supposed to know how to tell a great kid from a lemon?"

"Don't ask me," Roni said. "I only baby-sit my own family or close friends. I've never answered an ad in the newspaper in my life."

"Me neither," Ginger agreed. "The only baby-sitting jobs I've had have been for people I know."

"Well, unfortunately I've grown up deprived of normal social contacts," I said. "Sagebrush Academy was on top of a mountain with nothing around it but birds and lizards. And none of the girls there needed to baby-sit anyway."

"We'll try to help, Justine," Karen said, picking up the newspaper, "but I don't see how you can really tell much from an ad."

"Well, first of all it has to be in her part of town," Ginger said, wagging her sandwich at us. "She can't drive, and her stepmom might not feel well enough to drive her right now."

"Good point," I agreed. I didn't add that my part of town had all the best neighborhoods anyway— exactly what I was looking for. I didn't think I'd know how to baby-sit average kids.

"And it has to be someone who just wants after-school care," Roni added, peering over Ginger's shoulder at the paper. "Lots of these people want full-time child care while they're working."

"I think we should look for an ad that says baby-sitting, not child care," Karen suggested. "Child care implies that they want someone qualified, like a real nanny."

"I'm qualified," I said.

The other three burst out laughing. "Justine, when have you ever baby-sat in your life?" Ginger demanded.

"I helped out at the Country Club Christmas party last year," I said. "I handed out the gifts to the little kids. And I've helped Roni watch her little brother."

"Yeah, and you lost him the first time I left you alone with him," Roni quipped. "Don't get carried away, Justine. Find yourself one easy kid to start with, and just at night so the baby's ready for bed. You don't want to get stuck feeding it."

"Or diapering," I said, shuddering. "You're right."

"You're going to have to diaper, Justine," Ginger said.

"What age do they become potty trained?"

"Around two?" Roni suggested.

"Then I'll look for a two-year-old."

"The terrible twos?" Karen asked.

"Don't keep trying to put me off. I want this job, and I'm going to find the perfect child," I said. "Now keep looking."

They started studying the long column of want ads. There were a lot of desperate people in the city.

"Here's one," Ginger said. "Gentle, caring person needed to share our joy in our adorable, sensitive son."

Roni shook her head firmly. "Not that one," she said. "If parents think their child is adorable, he's usually a monster. And if they say sensitive, he's a crybaby."

"You're right," Ginger agreed. "How about this one? Lively two-year-old needs—"

"Lively also means he's a monster," Roni cut in.

"There have to be some sweet, quiet children in greater Phoenix," I complained. "Keep looking."

"Hey, this might be okay," Ginger said.

I looked where she was pointing. "Occasional evening care for baby boy," I read.

"And the phone number is pretty close to yours," Ginger added, "so it must be in your neighborhood."

"Yeah," I said, studying it. I could handle one baby boy, no sweat. By the time lunch was over I had found two more possibilities.

"Just think: before the day is over, I'll be an employed person," I said to my friends as we headed to class. It sounded strange even to me. Justine Craft, working for money? That was definitely a first! But I liked the sound of it. For the first time

48

in my life, I'd have my own money, not a charge card my father paid, not an allowance someone gave me, but my own money! Maybe I'd use it to buy a present for the baby. Then it would come entirely from me and nobody else. I liked that idea.

I couldn't wait to get home and find a job. I wriggled around in my seat all afternoon. My teachers kept asking if something was wrong, but I ignored them. What was school compared to getting your first baby-sitting job?

I ran out of last-period math class so quickly that I collided with Danny in the doorway and had to shove him out of the way. "Sorry, can't stop. Off to work," I called to him. I hoped he noticed how carefree I sounded.

When I got home, I sat next to the phone for a while, planning what to say. I had to sound mature and responsible. I practiced my speech in five or six different voices. Then I dialed the first number. The ad said, "Mother's helper wanted immediately."

If they wanted someone right away, maybe they wouldn't be too fussy about references and experience. After all, I had neither.

Someone picked up the phone. The first thing I heard was a kid screaming in the background. "Hi!

I'm calling about the baby-sitting job," I said. That came out pretty well—smooth and mature. I felt better already.

"Oh, thank heavens," cried the woman at the other end of the line. "How soon can you get here? My last girl left and I've had such bad luck trying to find a replacement. Put that down, Timmy. No, not on the baby! Jenny, stop pulling the kitty's tail! He's going to—" There was a scream, a crash, a loud meow, and then silence. "Sorry," the woman said breathlessly. "When did you say you could be here?"

"I think I've got the wrong number," I said quickly, slamming down the phone. What a close call! Two little kids *and* a psycho cat? Even their mother didn't seem to know what to do with them. I stared at the phone, half expecting it to ring and hear that woman's voice on the other end. "I've found you and you're not getting away!" she'd yell.

The phone rang, and I jumped. I almost didn't answer it until I told myself that I was being stupid.

"Justine?" Karen's voice demanded. "What took you so long to answer? Listen, I was proofreading the next edition of the school newspaper and there's someone looking for a baby-sitter in the want ads. I don't think it's too far from you."

"How many children?" I asked suspiciously. "Any pets?"

"Didn't say."

"I don't know, Karen. I just escaped the worst baby-sitting job in history."

"You do still want to baby-sit, don't you?"

"I guess," I said slowly. "Okay, give me the number. It couldn't be worse than the one I just talked to."

I scribbled down the number, then I called right away, before I lost my nerve.

"How very nice to get a reply so quickly." The voice sounded okay. Sort of precise, like a teacher. There was no screaming. "Tristan is so looking forward to this. I can't give him the time he needs, because I teach at Arizona State and I have a great deal of preparation to do in the evenings."

"Uh . . . how old is . . . uh, Tristan?"

"He's two and a half, a very bright little boy. What we're looking for is someone to keep him amused and challenged. When could you come over and meet Tristan?"

"Right away, if you like," I said. How bad could it be? Even I could keep a two-and-a-half-year-old amused.

I was out the front door in a flash, heading for a

house only three blocks away. This was working out just fine. Soon it would be me and Tristan, hanging out, having fun. Maybe I'd even tell Danny that I was spending every evening with a boy named Tristan!

Tristan's mother looked exactly the way I expected a college professor to look—serious and proper, but okay. No fashion sense, of course. But you couldn't expect that from a professor! Maybe if I was around long enough, I could help her improve her image.

"Please come in," she said. "Tristan is waiting for you in his playroom."

Tristan looked up as I walked in. He was dark haired and serious and he reminded me of someone . . . but I couldn't decide who.

"Hi, Tristan," I cooed in my best baby-sitter voice. "I'm Justine. I've come to play with you." Since he didn't say anything, I squatted down on the floor beside the toy chest. "What do you want to play?" I asked, picking up a stuffed toy. "Is this a big fierce dinosaur?"

He stared at me so long and so hard, I began to wonder if he couldn't talk yet or if he was about to throw up on me.

Then he said, "That's a *Tyrannosaurus rex*. You don't play with him. He's a carnivore." He looked disgusted by my ignorance.

"Oh—okay," I stammered. "What do you want to play with, then?"

"Are you good at computer games?" he asked. "I'm very good at computer games, right, Mommy?"

"Tristan, don't boast. It's not nice," his mother said.

"Well, I'm not too great," I stammered.

"Tristan, why don't you show Justine your newest game," his mother suggested.

Tristan climbed up on the chair. "Do you have CD-ROM?" he asked, calmly sliding in a disk as if he was an old pro. "We do. My brother has a program to fly a plane. This one lets you go inside someone's body. It's cool."

Tristan was just about to show me how his program worked when a door slammed and a voice called, "Mother, I'm home."

The door opened and in walked Walter the nerd. He looked at me in surprise. "Justine! What are you doing here?"

In one horrible flash, everything was clear. No wonder the kid was a pint-size genius. I was in the home of the biggest computer geek at Alta Mesa. I was baby-sitting a mini-nerd!

"I'm sorry," I stammered, getting hastily to my

feet, "but I don't think this is going to work. I'm not the person you need for your son. I'd just hold him back from winning the Nobel Prize at age four. I really should be going. Nice meeting you, Tris."

"Tristan," he said, still frowning at me. "My name is Tristan, like the opera, not Tris."

I fled, and I never looked back.

# Chapter 5

I didn't stop running until I got home. What a narrow escape! To think I might have been babysitting a nerd in training and not found out who he was for weeks. I could have actually been home alone with the mini-geek when Walter brought the nerd pack to visit. I felt hot all over just thinking of the awful possibilities.

At first I thought I'd never forgive Karen, but then I realized she had no way of knowing that a nerd had placed the ad in the school paper. Some nerve! How dare he do that without a disclaimer that the ad placer was a nerd? There should be a law about that!

I studied the newspaper again. I was almost

afraid to call the other numbers I'd circled. Who knew what horrors might be waiting for me? Then one ad caught my eye. At the top it read PARADISE VALLEY. That was a good start, because Paradise Valley is the most expensive neighborhood around here. Everybody drives a Mercedes or a Beemer. Everybody belongs to a country club. It's my kind of neighborhood! There's no way they would let nerds live in Paradise Valley, I was sure.

The ad read, "College student needed for afternoon child care. Mature and experienced only."

"Perfect," I whispered to myself. Okay, so there were some *slight* problems. I wasn't a college student and I wasn't exactly mature or experienced. But a Paradise Valley house would have cooks and maids hanging around who could help out if I needed them. With any luck, they'd even do the messy stuff like feeding and diapering. I wasn't sure why a family in Paradise Valley wanted a student instead of a professional nanny, but there had to be a good reason. Anyway, it was worth a try.

I dialed the number and put on a deep, smooth voice. "I'm applying for the position advertised in today's newspaper. Is it still open?"

I couldn't believe how perfectly the phone conversation went. There were no crying babies in the background. The mother sounded pleasant and normal. She asked when she could meet me and I said, "Right away! I live in the neighborhood."

That was obviously a plus point for her. I could understand why. It was only natural that she'd want her child taken care of by someone who knew the right brands of clothing and had grown up with the same imported designer toys.

"Wonderful," she cooed. "We'll see you in a few minutes."

I realized the first flaw in my plan as soon as I put the phone down. She was expecting me to drive, and there was no way I could get to the house in a few minutes on foot. *Think fast,* I told myself. *Call someone and ask for a ride! But who? Call a taxi! But that would look weird.*

Then it hit me—my bike! I still had a bike somewhere at the back of the garage. If I rode it over to her house, I could say I was saving the environment by not polluting the air with car exhaust. College students were into things like that.

That reminded me of the second flaw in my plan. Was I actually going to tell her I was a college student? I didn't think I could tell that big a lie. What if she found out and sued me for misrepresentation or something? But I'm a very creative person. I knew just what to do. I'd tell her something *close* to the truth. I'd say I was a high school senior, but very mature for my age. After all, she wasn't likely to know anyone at Alta Mesa. Most people in our kind of neighborhood sent their kids to private schools.

Now all I needed was a mature, collegiate image. Luckily Christine was still out at a doctor's appointment. I ran up to her bedroom and raided her closet for an Anne Klein jacket and Hermés silk scarf. I put them on and studied myself in her mirror. The clothes looked fine, but the face and hair still looked very high school. I yanked the ponytail out of my hair. There wasn't much else I could do with it in a hurry, so it hung around my shoulders, making me look like Alice in Wonderland. If Karen or Roni had been here, they could have French-braided it for me, or tried to get it into a twist. But there was no time to call them.

I decided to leave it down. If I was one of those ecology-minded students, then the natural look would be in. Oops! That meant no Anne Klein. I dug through Christine's drawers again and found a Sierra Club T-shirt with whales on it. I added her khaki walking shorts. Very earthy! And I didn't feel bad about borrowing them, because Christine was so big right now, she couldn't fit into them anyway.

It took a long time to find the bike way back behind last year's Christmas ornaments and the skis. Then it took a while longer to dust it off and pump up the flat tires. But when it was finally done, I put on my backpack and decided that I could pass very easily for an environmentally minded high school senior.

*Here goes nothing,* I said to myself as I swung onto the bike. I don't think I'd actually ridden it since I was about ten. I wobbled a lot, and I was glad that nobody was watching me ride off down my block. But luckily I'm very athletic and coordinated. All my ballet and fencing obviously paid off, because I arrived at the Paradise Valley house with knees pumping, looking like an Olympic cycling champion (if I do say so myself).

The woman I'd spoken to was looking out the front window as I rode up. The security gate across the driveway swung open for me, and I wheeled the bike up to a huge, two-story Tudor house. I couldn't remember how to work the kickstand, so I left the bike propped against a bush and jogged confidently over to the front door.

When the door opened, I was thrilled to see what my hopefully future-employer looked like.

She was slim and fit and, best of all, she was wearing a tennis outfit.

"Oh, you play tennis! That's great," I heard myself saying. It wasn't the right sort of opener for an employee, but it just slipped out. She smiled.

"You do too?"

I nodded. "They offered me a scholarship to Sandhurst to play tennis."

"Oh," she said, nodding appreciatively. "You must be pretty good. I'm afraid I'm just a beginner. I need help with my backhand."

"I'd be happy to give you tips," I said. This was going just great.

Then I noticed that her smile was fading.

"You have come about the baby-sitting job, right?"

I nodded.

"You look awfully young," she said suspiciously.

"That's always a big problem for me," I babbled cheerfully, "although my stepmother keeps telling me I'll be glad when I'm thirty and I only look twenty."

She smiled again. "Which college are you attending?"

"I'm not actually going to college yet," I said, feeling a blush creep up my cheeks. I willed myself to stop it. "But I'm planning to go back east to study ecology. I'm very mature for my age. And I really want this job."

She nodded. "Do you have references?"

"Oh yes," I lied, but inside I was starting to panic. Where would I get references from? What if she asked me for names or letters of recommendation? But suddenly she stuck out her hand. "I'm Melanie Holmes."

She hadn't told me her name before, and I hadn't even thought about it. Now I wished I'd thought up a fake name for myself. It was all too possible that she knew my father or belonged to our country club. But I couldn't think of one now.

"I'm Justine," I said.

"Well, Justine," she said, "what I'm looking for is a reliable person who can be here every afternoon. Our nanny has started taking classes at the community college. She's gone from three to six every day, so that's when I'll need you. I attend many charity meetings in the afternoon. Would you care to come inside and meet my children? Cassidy should be waking up from her nap about now."

She didn't wait for an answer. My heart was beating very fast as she led me into a gorgeous marble entrance hall, up a curved staircase, and into a nursery

61

that looked as if it belonged in Buckingham Palace. An adorable little girl was lying in a white wooden bed, her long dark curls spilling over the lace pillow. She looked soft and pink and cuddly. In fact, she was exactly the little angel I had pictured in my most perfect fantasy. I couldn't believe my luck!

"Cassidy," her mother whispered, "I've brought a new friend to see you."

Cassidy opened her eyes and held out her arms for her mother to pick her up. "Mama," she said in a cute little voice. She was wearing a pink-and-white gingham dress with a teddy bear embroidered on the front. I felt myself melting inside.

Mrs. Holmes glanced at me. "I'm afraid she's kind of clingy at the moment. She's having a hard time adjusting to her new baby sister." She tried to unwrap Cassidy's arms from her neck. "Cass, this is Justine. Would you like her to come play with you every day?"

Cassidy peeked at me from her mother's arms. "Okay," she said, her eyes big and serious. I gave her what I hoped was a reassuring smile.

"Do you have time to stay awhile now?" Mrs. Holmes asked me. "I really have a million things I should be doing."

"I can stay," I said. "Cassidy and I will have fun together, right, Cassidy?"

"Wonderful," Mrs. Holmes said. "I'd better show you Chloe's room. She usually sleeps until almost five. Then you can get her up and put her in the playpen. It might be wise not to put her where Cassidy can climb all over her."

"Okay," I said, still trying to sound calm and confident. But in a minute I would be alone with two little kids, one of whom didn't like the other very much. What would I do if the baby woke and started crying? Was I supposed to make formula? Didn't you have to sterilize bottles or something? What about dirty diapers? Suppose Mrs. Holmes came back and the diaper was pinned all wrong?

"This is splendid," she said, untangling Cassidy and handing her to me. "I'll see you later. Have fun, Cassidy, and be a good girl."

She fled before I could say a word. More than anything, I wished I could run after her. I glanced nervously at Cassidy, hoping she'd just look at me admiringly.

The adorable little angel took a very big breath, flung herself in the direction of the stairs, and screamed, *"Mommmmy!"*

# Chapter

## 6

I barely managed to hold onto Cassidy. I never knew little girls could be so strong! Once I had dragged her back to her room, she flung herself on the floor and started kicking wildly, screaming for her mother the entire time.

So much for the little angel! "Mommy will be back soon," I said. "Why don't you show me your toys, Cassidy?" I went to the toy box and started taking out toys. "Look at this, Cassidy!" I kept on talking without getting any response from her. "Is this your panda bear? Is this your dolly?" I tried to give the toys to Cassidy, but she kept hurling them away. When I offered her a plastic elephant, Cassidy flung it across the room. It bounced off the wall, missing the lamp by inches. I half-expected Mrs. Holmes to come running back, telling me I was fired. Why did I even want this job? If all kids were like this, then forget it.

But there was nothing I could do. After I finally got Cassidy to stop crying, she began grabbing everything from the floor and yelling, "Mine!" I couldn't get her to say anything else. The worst part was that after she had claimed a toy, she'd throw it across the room just as before.

Then a brilliant idea suddenly came to me. What did *I* do when I was bored and angry? I ate ice cream. Maybe that worked on little kids too. The kid couldn't yell if her mouth was full.

"You want something to eat, Cassidy?" I asked. "You want me to get you a cookie?"

"Okay," she said.

See, it was simple to get around little kids. "I'll be right back," I said. I went downstairs and found the kitchen. There was no sign of a cook. I located the cookie jar and came upstairs again with animal crackers and milk. *These should keep the little darling occupied for quite a while,* I thought.

"Here are the cookies, Cassidy," I began, but my voice trailed off as I realized I was talking to an empty room. "Cassidy?" I called. "Where are you . . . Cassidy?

66

Ohmygosh!" I put down the tray and sprinted to the baby's room. Chloe was lying in her crib, fast asleep. I breathed a huge sigh of relief. But the feeling only lasted a second. Cassidy stood by the window (which fortunately had bars over it), pushing all of the baby's things out and squealing with delight as they fell to the patio below.

I imagined Mrs. Holmes coming home and dying of heart failure when she saw splattered toys and baby powder and rattles lying all over the backyard.

"You come with me, young lady," I said, taking Cassidy's hand. "We're going to put you where you can't do any harm."

I led her, kicking and squirming, back to her bedroom. "Look, I brought you cookies," I said. "Now you sit at your table like a good girl while I go get your sister's toys."

I closed the door to the baby's room and sprinted down the stairs. This job was certainly not restful. Outside, I gathered up everything as quickly as I could, blew away the spilled powder, and headed back to the house. I reached to push open the back door.

It didn't move.

I put down the toys and tried to turn the handle.

Nothing. Shielding my eyes from the sun, I peeked through the glass door. There was Cassidy, a triumphant grin on her face. The little brat had locked me out!

"Cassidy," I commanded. "Open this door at once."

That didn't work. So I tried pleading. "Cassidy, please open the door right now. Open the door right now, Cassidy, or Justine will be mad at you . . . I'll tell your mommy you were a bad girl . . ."

That was no good. The last thing I wanted was for Mrs. Holmes to drive up and find me locked out while Cassidy did goodness knows what to the baby. I *had* to get back into that house!

"Cassidy, please show me what a big girl you are and open the door," I begged. "If you do, Justine will give you a surprise. I'll get you a big bowl of ice cream . . . I'll let you watch your favorite show on TV, okay?"

The door still didn't open. I was frantic now. When I peeked in again, I couldn't even see her. That had to mean she was somewhere she shouldn't be. Desperate, I started walking around the house, looking for any other doors, or a way in from the garage, or an open window. But the entire ground floor was locked up tight. Any second now I expected to hear a terrifying wail from the baby's room. I felt like crying myself.

Then I noticed a window open just a crack. It was a small window, probably a bathroom, on the second floor. Next to it was a balcony. And next to the balcony was a creeper climbing up the wall of the house. If I could climb that vine to the balcony, I'd be set!

I had never done too well with the ropes in gym, but I had been on the Matterhorn in the Alps once. Okay, so it hadn't exactly been climbing, but it was pretty steep walking. That must count, right? If I hadn't been so desperate, I would have known how crazy this idea was, but it was the only idea I had right now and time was precious. I couldn't decide which scenario was worse: Cassidy attacking her baby sister, or Mrs. Holmes coming back and finding me standing all alone outside.

I tested the creeper with a sharp tug. Loose leaves and twigs fell onto me, reminding me that *things* might live in a creeper . . . things like scorpions and spiders and lizards.

*Be brave, Justine,* I told myself.

I found a hold and started to climb. It was an old creeper, and the lower branches were big and solid. I got up the first few feet easily enough. For someone who had never been a tomboy, I wasn't doing too badly. If Ginger were here, she'd have been up this thing like a monkey. Ginger was still trying to shake off her tomboy image. But I had always been all girl. I had run to the housekeeper to have my hands wiped if they got dirty. I'd always worn dresses, and I'd never climbed trees.

Higher and higher I went, feeling more confident all the time. I felt like a hero in an action movie. Any minute now, I'd swing inside that window and save the baby, and everything would be okay. I plunged my hand into a big cobweb. I yelled, swung out from the wall, and slithered down a few feet until I managed to grab a thick branch.

That had been too close. I wasn't sure I wanted to go any higher, knowing that the owner of that large cobweb was probably waiting for me, watching me with her beady little spider eyes. But I had to do it. *Crafts never quit in the face of danger,* I told myself. There was a Craft in the Revolutionary War and one at Gettysburg, and they didn't quit. They died, but they didn't quit.

I leaned out from the leaves to see how I could go on up, but I'd slipped sideways and I couldn't find the right branch to grab. *Okay, go back down and start again,* I told myself, fighting to keep calm.

That was when I found that I couldn't go back down. Someone seemed to have wiped out all the footholds below me. I was stranded in the middle of a vine, on the middle of the wall, all alone. Now I wished I could *find* the hero of an action movie! I felt like calling for help, but I stopped myself. Even if anyone could hear me, I wouldn't want them to know what I was doing halfway up a wall. I took a deep breath and tried to think.

"Freeze! Hold it right there!"

The deep voice spoke right below me, surprising me so much I almost let go of the branch. I managed to turn enough to look over my shoulder, and then I almost lost my grip again.

I was staring into the eyes of the most gorgeous guy I had ever seen.

# Chapter 7

"Hold it right there," he repeated. "Don't try to move."

*How sweet,* I thought. *He's come to rescue me.* Somehow this adorable guy had seen that I was in trouble and come to my aid. I wouldn't have been surprised if he'd been wearing a cape. He was actually wearing denim shorts and a turquoise tank top with Timberland boat shoes—which you have to admit is a more hip outfit than any old cape!

"Okay, back on down," he commanded.

"I would if I could," I called. "I'm kind of stuck."

He climbed up behind me as easily as Tarzan. Although from what I could see over my shoulder, he was better looking than Tarzan, and definitely better dressed.

"Put your left foot here," he said, tapping my left ankle and guiding it to a fork in the trunk of the vine. "Now lower yourself to here . . ."

I was on the ground beside him in no time. Now that I could see him close up, I decided I had underestimated how gorgeous he really was. He had dark wavy hair, the longest eyelashes I've ever seen on a guy, and the sort of strong chin with a cleft in it that you only see in cologne commercials. But it was his eyes that were the most amazing. They were almost violet, and they flashed as he looked at me.

"Thanks a million," I gasped, as much from the shock of being close to a mega-hunk as from relief at getting back down to the ground. "You saved my life."

He was giving me a hard, cold stare. "You're lucky I didn't leave you where you were," he said. "You deserve to be stranded up there."

"Okay, I know it was dumb of me to try it," I said, "but it was the only way in."

His eyes registered surprise. "You're actually admitting to me that you were trying to get into the house?"

"Sure," I said. "I was planning to try and get in through that open window."

His eyes shot wide open in amazement. "Wow, talk about cool," he said. "I suppose I should admire your honesty, but don't think it will stop me from calling the cops."

"What?"

"You were going to break into this house. You just admitted it! You don't think I'm going to let you off, do you? For all I know, you could be the burglar who's been working this neighborhood for months."

I didn't think I was hearing right. I was so surprised that for once in my life I was speechless. The guy went on. "No one ever thought the burglar could be a girl. This will really blow them away."

"Wait a sec—" I tried to interrupt, but he was on a roll now.

"It's always the same method, isn't it? Watch the house, wait until the owner leaves, and then a quick entry into the master suite and out with the jewelry. Although I don't know how you managed to make it past the Holmeses' security system. They thought it was foolproof."

I was hot all over from embarrassment, but also from anger. This jerk thought I was a burglar!

"For your information," I said coldly, "I got through the security system because Mrs. Holmes opened the gate for me."

He looked impressed. "And then you hung around until she left? You really *are* cool."

"And you really are stupid," I snapped. "Do I look like a burglar?"

He was watching me warily, his face hostile. "Maybe you're a messed-up kid who does it for kicks."

"Look," I said. "I'd love to stay here chatting with you, but I'm kind of in a crisis. I have to get into this house."

"No way!" he said. "If you're not a burglar, you'd better have a good explanation of what you were doing ten feet up the ivy."

I was beginning to panic again. After my shock at meeting this awesomely cute guy, it was just coming back to me why I was trying to break into the house in the first place. Who knew what Cassidy could be doing at this very moment! "I'm the new baby-sitter," I snapped.

"Oh," he said, the tough expression leaving his face for the first time. "Yeah, I remember Mrs. Holmes said she was trying to get an ASU student to help the nanny." Then he paused, studying me as if something was bothering him. "Okay," he said slowly, "so if you're the baby-sitter . . . why are you trying to break into the house?"

"Wait a minute, Mr. Detective," I said, "who are you? For all I know, *you* could be the serial burglar, just waiting to get rid of me so that you can climb in through the window yourself!"

He grinned, and the smile made him look much younger. "Touché," he said. "I'm J. P. McPherson— I live next door. I saw you climbing up the wall from my backyard, so I figured I'd be a hero and catch you single-handedly."

"That was very brave of you," I said. "But weren't you taking a big risk? If I really was the burglar, I might be dangerous."

He smiled even wider. "I think I could handle you," he said.

"I might be an expert at karate."

"I have a black belt."

"I might have had a gun on me."

"I doubt it," he said.

I found myself blushing. "This is stupid," I said. "If you really are the next-door neighbor, then for pete's sake, help me get into the house."

"What's wrong with the door?"

"It's locked."

He grinned again. "You locked yourself out?"

"Correction: Cassidy locked me out. She threw toys out the window, and when I went down to get them, she locked the door behind me. At this moment she's probably hitting her sister with a heavy piece of furniture."

"Oh, no," J.P. said. "Hold on a second—we've got a spare key. I'll be right back."

He sprinted across the patio and disappeared down a side path. I watched him, feeling very confused. It wasn't every day that someone who looked like Superman, only better, swung himself up a vine beside me, helped me to safety, and then tried to arrest me.

But I didn't have long to ponder this, because he was back in no time at all, waving a key triumphantly.

"Now we'll just have to hope the little brat didn't put the chain on the front door," he said, running up the steps. Miraculously, the door swung open. We both raced up the stairs yelling "Cassidy!"

The house was silent. We pushed open the baby's door. The crib was empty.

"Oh no!" J.P. and I said at the same time.

We both swung around as we heard a noise. Cassidy was standing in the doorway with a little smile on her face.

"Hi, J.P.," she said.

"Cassidy, honey," I said, trying to sound calm. "What have you done with the baby?"

"Baby's hiding," she said.

"What?"

"Baby's playing hide-and-go-seek with me."

I was across that room in a second. I knelt down and grabbed her shoulders. "Listen here, you little brat, where did you put the baby?"

J.P. tapped me on the shoulder. "I don't think that will work," he said. "She's a stubborn little kid. I've baby-sat her before." He knelt down beside Cassidy. "Okay, Cass. We'll play hide-and-go-seek with you," he said, making eye contact with me over Cassidy's head. He started walking toward the baby's closet. "Are we getting warm?"

Cassidy shook her head. "Very, very cold," she said delightedly. "You're soooo cold."

"Stay calm," J.P. muttered to me. "She's only a little kid. She couldn't have carried the baby far."

"She could have dropped her down the stairs."

"We'd have heard crying."

Just as he said that, we heard a sort of hiccuping cry coming from across the hall. We glanced at each other and sprinted into Cassidy's room. The baby was lying in the doll's cradle, surrounded by stuffed animals.

When she saw us, she started to cry. I snatched her up and she cried even louder.

"You didn't play fair, Chloe," Cassidy yelled. "I told you not to make a noise."

"You were very bad to move the baby like that, Cassidy," J.P. said. "And you were very bad to lock the door on your baby-sitter . . ." He looked at me in an almost friendly way for the first time. "I don't even know your name."

"It's Justine," I said.

"You were very mean to Justine," J.P. said. "She won't ever come back again to play with you if you act up like that. Now start putting all those toys away before your mommy gets back."

"No!" Cassidy said defiantly.

"I'm counting to three, Cassidy."

"You're mean. I hate you," Cassidy yelled.

"I know," J.P. said with a grin. "Okay, let's have a contest. Let's see who can throw the toys into the toy box first. Ready, go."

To my amazement Cassidy started picking up toys and throwing them into her toy box. J.P. gave me a wink.

"How did you do that?" I asked.

"Experience. I have two younger brothers," he said, smiling.

I could have stood there looking into those incredible eyes forever, but I forced myself to remember that I was supposed to be responsible here.

"I left all the baby's stuff outside the back door," I said. "I'd better go get it."

"I'll get it," J.P. said. "You put the baby back to bed . . . and it smells like she needs changing."

I didn't have any choice. I actually had to change a diaper. And I have to tell you, it was totally gross—I nearly barfed a couple of times. But then, just when I was wiping her little bottom with a baby wipe, she gave me a big smile that made her whole body wriggle. It was so sweet that I forgot the disgusting diaper. I tickled her and played with her and she went right on grinning and giggling and being totally adorable.

I was just putting on the new diaper (a disposable one with tabs, so that even a dope like me could see how to do it) when J.P. came back in with the load of baby things he'd found.

"She seems to like you," he commented as the baby went on giggling.

"At least I've made one friend today. One out of three isn't bad, I suppose."

"Three?"

"You and Cassidy haven't exactly been charming to me."

"Well, you and I met under strange circumstances," he said, looking at me appraisingly, "and Cassidy's mad at the world right now. You might want to have a word with her."

"About what?"

"Isn't it obvious?" he said sharply. "The kid's being eaten up with jealousy. She just needs to know that she's still wanted around here."

"Oh," I said.

I put the baby in her playpen and followed J.P. into Cassidy's room. She had lost interest in putting away her toys and was squatting on the floor, doing a puzzle.

"Cassidy, I want you to listen to me," J.P. said.

Cassidy turned away. "No," she yelled.

J.P. sat down next to her. "You're going to listen whether you like it or not," he said. "What you did to the baby was very, very bad. You could have hurt her."

Cassidy glared up at J.P. "Don't care," she said.

"But, Cassidy, she's your little sister," I added. "You have to take care of her. You're the big sister now."

"No little sister," she snapped.

"Listen to me," J.P. began, but she turned away from him. I could sense she was about to launch into hysterics again.

"Let me," I said. I knelt down beside her. "Listen, Cassidy," I said gently. "I know you're mad at your mommy and daddy for bringing a new baby into the house. And I know you don't like the baby right now. But you have to understand, this baby is here to stay, and you can't change that."

When I heard my words, it was as if someone had hit me over the head. Suddenly I realized that I could have been talking to myself. I'd been jealous too, and scared that I wouldn't matter once the baby arrived.

J.P. took Cassidy's hand. "Chloe's part of your family now and you all belong together," he said. "But your mom and dad still love you just as much. Understand?"

Cassidy nodded, but I was the one who felt my eyes filling with tears. Everything J.P. said was true. Nothing would change between Dad and Christine and me. They'd never been the most loving parents in the first place, but they cared for me in their own way. And the new baby was going to be part of our family whether I liked it or not. So it was up to me to make the best of it. And if our baby smiled at me the way baby Chloe had, I didn't think it would be too hard.

"I better get going," J.P. said, getting to his feet. "I was on my way to meet some friends from college at Fiddler's Dream over in Tempe. It's a neat place. Do you ever go there?"

"It's a little far for me," I said without thinking.

"It only takes ten minutes if it's not rush hour."

"In a car, yes."

He looked at me in surprise. "You don't drive?"

I'd had so many traumas in the last thirty minutes that I'd let my guard down. I realized at the last second that I was about to walk into a trap.

"I . . . uh . . . I'm into saving the environment," I blurted.

He looked at the whales on my T-shirt and nodded. "Good thought," he said. "But what happens when you need to get somewhere farther away? How do you get to classes?"

I could hardly say I had my dad or stepmom drive me. "I work it out somehow," I said. "You know, car pools. They're good."

He grinned. He really did have the most wonderful smile. "Sorry, but I love my little yellow Porsche too much to give it up, even to save the environment."

All I could do was smile like a dolt.

"I've gotta run, Justine, but I'll see you around—
*if* you don't get yourself fired for losing the baby."

"Don't worry," I said. "Now that I know what
adorable little girls can do, I'm going to watch her
like a hawk, right, Cassidy?"

Cassidy glared at me so fiercely that I laughed.
Then she smiled too. "I think Cassidy and I are
going to get along just fine," I said.

"See ya, then," J.P. said. He gave a friendly wave.
"Bye, Cass."

Cassidy stuck out her tongue. J.P. laughed as he
ran back down the stairs. As I watched him go, I
found that my heart was racing. Drop-dead cute
*and* a little yellow Porsche? I had just found my
dream guy!

# Chapter

## 8

I don't even remember getting home. The pedals just seemed to turn with no effort at all. Before I knew it, I was flying down the twilight streets, the wind in my face and my thoughts floating up to those pink clouds above my head. I couldn't wait to get to the phone and call my friends. I could just imagine how they'd drool with envy when I told them that I'd met my dream boy—just as I'd described him, including the yellow Porsche. They probably wouldn't even believe me at first. I have been known to exaggerate at times, just a little.

But when they finally realized I was telling the truth, they'd be so impressed! And Danny too. Wouldn't he be mad when he heard that I'd found someone so much cooler than him! Somehow I'd have to get a photo of J.P. and casually pass it around in class at school. Maybe I could bring my camera with me the next time I baby-sat. Wow! I'd have to tell my friends about my new job, too! I bet they'd be impressed with the way I conned myself into the perfect baby-sitting job.

I'd been so cool—apart from getting locked out and losing the baby and having to change a diaper, I mean. Mrs. Holmes had seemed pretty happy when she came home.

"How did everything go?" she'd asked nervously after sprinting up the stairs to make sure the baby was still in one piece.

"Oh, just fine," I'd said without blushing. "Everything went just fine."

"Nothing happened?" She was still looking around nervously, but I'd put everything back where it came from.

"Nothing special," I'd said. "Cassidy and I played with her dolls. I changed the baby's diaper." I glanced across at Cassidy, wondering if she was going to say anything, but we'd had a tea party with real cookies and milk and we'd actually gotten along pretty well. Maybe she'd forgotten all about my earlier panic.

A big smile spread across Mrs. Holmes's face. I could see that she thought I was the best baby-sitter in the world. She asked me to come back every day that week.

I waved as I climbed onto my bike. She waved. Cassidy waved. I rode out of that security gate with a big grin on my face. I'd been a great baby-sitter. The baby had actually smiled at me! Okay, so Cassidy was going to be a challenge, but I understood where she was coming from now. We were in the same boat. I could help her see that being a big sister wasn't all bad.

And I was going to be next door to J.P. every day. We'd become friends and then maybe more than friends. I wished I knew more about him. Maybe that was a job for the Boyfriend Club. They could do some scouting around and find out his likes and dislikes. I'd have to ask when I talked to them. . . .

I was in a big rush to call them, which was probably why I took the turn into our driveway too quickly. One minute I was riding like a pro, the next the bike went flying out from under me and I slid across the gravel. I must have yelled, because the front door opened and Christine came waddling out.

"Justine! Are you okay?"

"I think so," I said, sitting up cautiously, "apart from having three thousand pieces of rock embedded in my flesh." I was joking, but as I looked at myself, I saw that it was true. My whole left side was red and bleeding and had bits of gravel stuck in it.

"Oh, Justine," Christine gasped. "Come on, let's get you into the house."

She helped me up and we staggered up the front steps together. "What on earth were you doing on a bike, anyway? I didn't even know you owned a bike."

"It was at the back of the garage, behind the Christmas stuff," I said. "I needed to get somewhere in a hurry, and you weren't home."

She looked scared and sick as she started getting out antiseptic and gauze pads from the downstairs bathroom cabinet. "Where did you have to go in such a hurry? Was it an emergency?"

"Not really," I said. "I had a job interview and I had to get there somehow."

"A job interview?"

"Yeah, I decided to get a baby-sitting job."

"Baby-sitting, right now? Justine, why would you do that? You're going to have your own little brother or sister to baby-sit in a couple of weeks."

"Exactly," I said. "I wanted some experience

before the baby arrived so I'd know what to do with it."

Her face just melted. "Justine, that is so sweet of you. What a wonderful big sister you'll make."

Any other time I'd have been barfing by now, but my leg was beginning to sting all over and someone being nice to me was too much to handle. I felt the tears well up and quickly squeezed them back.

"And this is how you get rewarded for your good intentions," she went on, gently sponging the scrapes with warm water. "That's really not fair, is it?"

"The pain's not too bad," I said bravely. "They're not deep cuts, just scrapes. It only *looks* gross." I had been busy thinking that meeting J.P. was my reward for my wonderful intentions. But then it hit me I looked gross. The next time I saw J.P., I'd have a leg that looked as if it came straight from the emergency room.

"Oh no," I wailed.

"Am I hurting you?" Christine stopped sponging.

"No, it's okay. It's just that I'm doomed to wear pants for the next month."

"Poor baby. We'll have to go out and buy you some loose silky pants so that they don't rub against your skin."

"Okay," I said. Really, this whole thing wasn't turning out too badly after all.

I let Christine help me into the kitchen and fix me dinner. She kept giving me encouraging smiles to let me know how wonderful I was.

"I'm really counting on you, Justine," she said as we sat down to shrimp salad together. "Your father is so busy at work right now that he's hardly home. And there's a rumor that he'll have to fly to London soon. I'd hate to have him away when the baby arrives. I'm so glad I've got you here." She reached across the table and covered my hand with hers.

This was the same woman who had a fit if I put my ice cream bowl down on her silk couch! The same woman who made me feel like an outsider when I dared to put a doll in her baby's crib. It looked as if finally they were beginning to realize that good old Justine was needed around here!

After supper Christine helped me up to my room. I lay back contentedly on my bed with my homework beside me. Apart from the minor disasters, it had been a good day. I was needed and appreciated, and I'd just met the future love of my life. True, J.P. hadn't exactly gazed at me as if he thought I might be the future love of *his* life, but we'd straighten that out soon. My fellow Boyfriend

Club members would know what to do. They always came up with good ideas, and this wouldn't even be a challenge for them. All they had to do was convince a gorgeous college guy with a yellow Porsche that a high school freshman with gravel burns all over her leg was the girl of his dreams!

I decided not to call them tonight after all, because I'd have to speak to them one at a time and we always worked best when we were all together. *Why don't we have conference calling,* I wondered. If Christine went on being nice to me, I might just ask her to pay for it. I fell asleep with a big smile on my face and I didn't even notice that my left leg was sore.

The next morning Christine offered to drive me to school, so I got there really early. I paced up and down past the lockers, willing my friends to hurry up and get there. Karen arrived first, as usual. Karen is always early.

"Hold it right there and don't move," I instructed her. As I said the words, memories of my first meeting with J.P. came flooding back to me. Those were his very words to me! It had to be fate that had brought us together. Or maybe it was Cupid, disguised as Cassidy. If it hadn't been for the little brat throwing things out the window, I'd never have met J.P. I would be grateful to that adorable little girl forever.

"What's wrong?" Karen asked, glancing around nervously. "There aren't any nerds around, are there?"

"I don't even care if there are," I said, smiling sweetly. "Today I'd even be nice to a nerd."

"Are you feeling okay?" Karen asked.

I nodded. "It's just that I've got something to tell you and I want to wait until the others are here."

"Your stepmom had the baby?"

"Way better than that!"

"What, then?"

"Not until the others get here."

Karen glared at me, but I just giggled. Then Roni and Ginger burst through the doors.

"Get over here, you guys," I yelled down the hall. "I've got an assignment for the Boyfriend Club."

"Justine!" Ginger said, glancing around. "Don't yell out things like that. People will think there really *is* a Boyfriend Club. They'll think we're totally juvenile."

"There *is*," I said. "And I need its services right now. I need to find out every detail about the guy I met—his favorite music, his favorite color, who his friends are, where he hangs out—"

"You met a new guy?" Ginger interrupted.

"I met *the* new guy," I said. "Remember I told you about my dream guy—how he'd be dark and gorgeous and drive a Porsche? Well, I've met him and you have to help me snag him."

"You met a guy who drives a Porsche?" Ginger demanded, looking impressed. "Hey, not bad. Where did you meet him?"

"My first afternoon at my new job. He lives next door."

"New job? What new job?" Roni demanded.

"I got a job yesterday. It is exactly the baby-sitting job I was looking for—Paradise Valley mansion with security gates, live-in nanny who goes to classes in the afternoons, *and* this guy J.P. living next door."

"Wow, Justine, way to go," Roni said. "So how did you find out he drives a Porsche? Did you see him drive up in it?"

"No, he told me. He said that was why he couldn't be environmentally correct, because he loves his car too much to give it up."

"You actually spoke to him?" Karen shrieked.

"Sure. We had a long conversation."

"How did you get to meet him?"

"He tried to arrest me for burglarizing—"

"What?"

"I was trying to climb into the house after the baby locked me out . . ."

For some reason they found this hysterically funny.

I waited for their laughter to stop. Then I told them all the details. They ate up every word until I mentioned that J.P. had invited me to meet him at Fiddler's Dream.

"That was when I made my big mistake," I told them. "He almost found out that I was a little high school student."

"Wait a minute," Karen interrupted. "Justine, are you trying to tell us that this guy thinks you're in college?"

"I didn't exactly say that," I said, feeling uncomfortable for the first time that morning. "But I think he assumed . . ."

"Why would he have done that, Justine?" Roni asked.

"Because Mrs. Holmes was advertising for a college student to baby-sit—"

"And you let her think you were in college?" Roni yelled.

"No, of course not," I said fiercely. "I knew I couldn't pull that off. But I did sort of hint that I was about to go to college in the fall."

"Justine!" they all yelled together.

"Well, what else could I do?" I demanded. "I wanted the job and she'd never have given it to me if she thought I was a freshman. And J.P. will never look at me twice if he thinks I'm a freshman either." I grabbed Roni and Karen, who were nearest to me. "Come on, guys, you've got to help me. I have to get J.P. to like me. If he's crazy about me, then he won't care if I'm in high school or not."

"Get real, Justine," Roni said. "A college guy is not going to want to date a high school kid. He's out of your league."

"I think you should forget about him right now, Justine," Karen said. "Roni's right. Besides, you're certainly not mature enough to date a college guy!"

"I'll have you know that I'm very mature for my age," I said, tossing back my ponytail. "At Sagebrush we grew up very fast. All that traveling turned us into sophisticated women."

This made them all start laughing again, which annoyed the heck out of me. "Okay," I said. "Don't help me. See if I care. But you're not going to stop me from going after J.P. in a big way. I'm going to get him to notice me or die in the attempt. And when I wave to you from his

Porsche on my way to the coffeehouses in Tempe, then you'll all burst with jealousy and we'll see who gets the last laugh!"

I pushed past them and strode off down the hall. And I didn't wait for them to catch up with me.

# Chapter 9

Later that day my friends tried to make it up to me. They were waiting for me when I came out of the bathroom at lunchtime.

"I'm sorry if we hurt your feelings, Justine," Karen said. "We didn't really mean to laugh at you. It's pretty obvious that this is serious stuff for you."

"We just don't want to see you get hurt," Roni said. "You always get these big ideas that are too much for you to handle."

"Yeah, Justine," Ginger added. "Remember the time you had a mega-crush on that motorcycle guy and you dragged us to that sleazy club in the middle of the night?"

"This is different," I said. "For one thing, I'm

older and wiser now, and for another, J.P. is the most amazing guy in the world. Nobody could find anything wrong with him—he's cute, he's brave, he's even great at climbing walls."

"Are you sure he doesn't wear a cape?" Karen asked with a grin.

"Are you sure he wasn't just a hallucination?" Ginger added. "He sounds too good to be true."

"He's real, believe me. Those muscles, those eyelashes . . ."

"Sounds like she got over Danny pretty quickly," Roni muttered.

"Danny who?" I asked brightly. Then it occurred to me that she was right. I'd done all this in the first place to stop myself from thinking about Danny. It had certainly worked—I hadn't thought about Danny once since I met J.P.

"I'm sure the age thing won't even matter, once we get to know each other," I said. "This is my kind of guy we're talking about. He's rich, he's cute, he drives my dream car. You have to help me."

"I don't know how we can help, Justine," Karen said hesitantly.

"Karen's right," Ginger said. "We don't know anybody who lives in snobby places like Paradise Valley and we don't know anybody who goes to

Arizona State, either. There's no way we can find out about him."

"Then I'm doomed," I said, using Roni's favorite expression.

She looked at me with understanding. "Maybe Karen could do something," she suggested.

"Me? Why me?" Karen asked.

"Because you know Damien Evans. If anyone at our school knew this J.P. guy, it would be Damien."

"Good thinking," I said. Damien was editor of the school newspaper and a really popular senior.

Karen nodded. "I could ask him. He knows an awful lot of people. And he does hang out in those coffeehouses in Tempe. He took me to one once." Karen had amazed us all by having an almost-romance with Damien. Now they worked together on the school newspaper.

"So that's step one," Roni said. "Karen will try to find out anything she can about J.P."

"Then step two has to be deciding on my image," I said. "I have to look like the kind of girl who would interest a college guy."

"Face it, Justine. You look like a freshman," Ginger said. "If you try to make yourself look older, you'll just end up looking stupid."

"But I can't just look like me!" I wailed. "Even if

I do have naturally beautiful blond hair and the best wardrobe at Alta Mesa—stop laughing, you guys, it's true. I can't help it if I'm gorgeous by nature."

"Then you have nothing to worry about," Ginger said. "Just be your normal gorgeous self and J.P. will notice you. Seems like he already has, if he carried you down from a wall."

"But he thought I was a burglar then. He didn't notice me for myself. Anyway, it's finding the right image more than the right clothes—I have to act like someone who's older. What do I know about college courses and SAT scores? Yesterday I pretended to be one of those environmental types because they don't wear makeup and they look young—"

"So keep doing that," Ginger interrupted. "You helped me save Spirit Rock and turn it into a nature preserve, so that gives you something to talk about."

"Yeah, that's a good idea, Justine," Karen said. "Wear hiking shorts and boots and you'll be fine, as long as he's not an outdoorsy type too."

"One small problem," I said. "I can't wear shorts anymore."

"Why not?"

"This," I said, and lifted my pant leg.

"Holy cow! What happened to you?" Ginger yelled.

"*Madre de Dios,* Justine, that looks awful," Roni agreed.

"My bike skidded on the gravel," I said.

"Bike? I didn't even know you had a bike," Karen said.

"Why does everyone keep saying that?" I moaned. "I was dying to get home and call you guys. That's why I took the corner too fast. It's okay. It doesn't hurt too much, but just look at my leg! It's disgusting."

"You could always say that you did it mountain biking," Ginger suggested.

"Ginger, that would be lying," Karen scolded.

"Not exactly. She fell off a bike. She could sort of hint that the bike was on a mountain at the time. That's a perfectly acceptable injury."

"I'd rather not let him find out about the injury at all," I said, "but if I have to show him, then mountain biking sounds good."

"I don't know about you, Justine." Karen shook her head. "Why can't you fall for a nice, normal boy instead of all these exotic ones?"

"I did have a nice, normal boyfriend, remember?" I said bitterly. "Look where it got me."

"I'm sorry," Karen said. "That was dumb of me. I personally think you're making a big mistake running after this college guy, but I guess I can understand how you feel. I'll ask Damien about J.P. today."

"Thanks," I said. I went to afternoon classes feeling hopeful. Damien was sure to have heard of J.P. And as soon as I knew all about him, I'd know how to get him interested in me.

That afternoon I stopped off at Banana Republic and got a pair of safari pants. They were baggy with pockets and they didn't rub against my leg. I also bought a T-shirt with wildflowers on it and hastily tried to learn their names before I headed over to the Holmes house. Christine offered to drive me, but I refused. I couldn't risk anyone seeing the independent environmentalist student being driven to work by her mommy.

Mrs. Holmes greeted me happily. Cassidy glared at me. And Chloe smiled and made cute baby noises. I glanced out her window as I played with her, but there was no sign of a yellow car in the next-door driveway.

I kept looking all afternoon while I tried to keep Cassidy amused. This wasn't easy, because she was still into the "mine" syndrome. But we had another tea party and played "going to the store," and she finally stopped saying "Mine" to everything I picked up.

"What you lookin' for?" she asked as I peeked out the window for the fiftieth time.

"I was seeing if it was time for your mommy to come home," I lied.

"Mommy's coming home," she said excitedly. She got her stool and knelt on it, looking for her mother's car. I peeked out too, trying to spot a little yellow Porsche. We looked all afternoon, and Cassidy eventually got to see her mom's car. But the one thing we didn't see was J.P. I rode home slowly and sadly.

I began to wonder if my friends were right and he really had been a hallucination. Even Damien Evans didn't know anything about him. Nobody knew anything about him. I wanted to ask my dad if he played golf with anyone called McPherson at the country club, but he was never around. He was still handling this major crisis at work and didn't get home until late every night.

On Thursday it was very hot. I arrived at the Holmes house to be met by Cassidy in her swimsuit. "Go baby pool, okay?" she demanded.

Mrs. Holmes appeared behind her. "She's been begging to go in the pool all afternoon, but I

105

haven't had time to watch her. Maybe you'd be an angel and take her in the water. Chloe's asleep and you can take the monitor down with you."

"I didn't bring my suit with me," I ventured. That wasn't exactly true, since I was actually wearing my bathing suit under my clothes. It had been so hot that I'd gone for a quick swim at home before coming over. But I didn't want to go swimming here. What if J.P. came over and saw my ugly leg?

Mrs. Holmes shook her head. "It's not necessary. She's only allowed in her own little pool, and it's just a foot deep. You just have to watch her. I won't be gone long."

"Okay," I said.

I took Cassidy's hand and she led me out to the baby pool. It was one of those plastic pools in the shape of a turtle, and it stood in the shade of a big palm tree at one end of the real swimming pool. Cassidy got in and started happily splashing with her toys. I sat in the shade, fanning myself with a plastic spade and wondering if I should just forget about J.P. and strip down to my own swimsuit. It certainly was hot. I pulled off my T-shirt and rolled up my pant legs as far as possible and went to sit at the side of the big pool, letting my feet dangle into the cool water.

That was much better. I leaned back and gazed up at the blue sky between the palm branches. *It's not a bad life being paid for this,* I thought. I started to plan what I was going to buy with the money I was making.

There was a loud splash right beside me.

"Cassidy!" I yelped. She stood behind me with a grin on her face, pointing to her big plastic dump truck, which now floated in the middle of the pool. "Cassidy, that's not nice," I said. She went on grinning. "You have to play in your own pool."

"No," she whined. "I want to swim in the big pool."

"You can't, because I don't have my suit on today. I'll bring it with me tomorrow and we can go swimming together, okay?"

"No, now," she insisted. I tried to lead her back to her pool, but she started crying. "I want my truck." She pointed at the rapidly sinking truck and started jumping up and down.

"It's your fault. You threw the truck in the pool," I said. Then, as she kept on crying, I relented. "Just be patient and I'll get it for you." I knelt at the edge and tried making waves to drive the truck to the other side. It worked, too! The truck bobbed its way across the pool. But before I could go around to rescue it, Cassidy ran to get it.

"Cassidy, wait! Don't do that. You might—" I was going to say "fall in," but I didn't have the chance. Cassidy reached out for the truck and toppled into six feet of water.

I'd taken a lifesaving course at Sagebrush, but I never dreamed I'd have to use it. Now I didn't have any choice. Cassidy was struggling in the water, thrashing away in the middle of the pool. I dove in, feeling the icy coolness surround me, and came up right behind her. I remembered everything—the right hold, the right things to say, the right way to swim while carrying someone. In a couple of seconds, I'd propelled her to the steps.

I looked up to see a shadow looming over me. My first thought was that it was Mrs. Holmes, back in time to witness the near drowning of her precious child. But when I looked into the bright sun, I saw J.P. towering over me. "Boy, that was pretty impressive," he said. "I vaulted the fence when I heard the splash, but you stole my glory. You've already saved her."

"Luckily I took a lifesaving class," I said, handing the whimpering child to J.P. and then climbing up the steps myself.

"So did I, but that was years and years ago," J.P. said. "Way back in freshman year of high school. I

108

don't know how you can still remember all that stuff."

"Good memory," I said. I stood there, dripping all over, water cascading from my sodden pant legs.

Cassidy was really crying now. "I felled in," she said.

"You're okay," J.P. comforted her. "Justine saved you."

I took Cassidy's hand. "Come on, Cassidy. Let's go get you dried off," I said. I wrapped her in her towel. "There, all better."

"You're the one who could use some drying off," J.P. said. "Life sure isn't dull when you're around, is it? One week with the family and this kid has probably had more excitement than she's had in her entire life. Are things always this dramatic around you?"

"Not usually," I said, trying to keep my dignity while water ran down my hair and into my eyes and my pants made a big puddle on the deck. "Usually my life is very boring. It's hardly my fault if I'm stuck with a kid from a horror movie to baby-sit."

"I don't remember all these accidents happening when Kirsten's looking after her," J.P. said, still grinning. "I wonder if Mrs. Holmes had a chance to check up on you. Are you sure you didn't forge your references? Did you tell her about all the kids you've lost so far?"

I could see he was teasing, but he obviously didn't know he was hitting on a nerve. "I've never had problems with a child until now," I said haughtily. That was true! Cassidy was the first child I'd ever baby-sat. "I only seem to have problems with Cassidy when you're around, so maybe you're the bad influence."

"Girls have said that about me before," he said, grinning wickedly.

Cassidy was still whining. "I want a cookie," she whimpered. "I want to go inside."

"I guess I have to get going," I said. "Thanks for coming over. If I hadn't known how to swim, we both would have drowned without you." What a dumb thing to say! I felt my cheeks turning pink.

"You better get out of those wet clothes before you go inside," J.P. said with an amused look on his face. "I don't think Mrs. Holmes would appreciate water spots all over her polished marble floor. Why aren't you in your bathing suit, anyway?"

"I didn't feel like swimming," I lied. I looked around. "I don't have a towel."

"Check the pool house," he suggested. "I'll watch Cassidy for a minute." There didn't seem to be any choice. I really couldn't go inside with these baggy pants dripping water. I headed into the little pool house, feeling like a dork. Why did J.P. always see me when I was at a disadvantage? I managed to get the wet pants off, and then I grabbed the biggest towel I could find. I wrapped it around my waist and hoped he wouldn't notice my cut-up leg.

"All set?" J.P. asked as I came out. Then he did a double take. "What happened to your leg?"

I thought of Ginger. "Mountain bike accident," I said. "That's why I was wearing pants."

He shook his head. "See, I was right! You *are* a walking disaster area!"

"I am not. It was a very hard trail."

"You certainly don't live a quiet life, I'll say that for you," he said. His eyes were teasing me, challenging, laughing.

Having him laugh at me was more than I could bear right now. The shock of rescuing Cassidy was just beginning to kick in, and my cuts were stinging from the chlorine in the water. "I have to go," I said. "I don't have time to plan any more embarrassing disasters for your amusement, but if you stick around, I'm sure I can arrange to fall off the roof or maybe set the house on fire next time." I

111

grabbed Cassidy's hand firmly, scooped up my wet pants, and started for the house.

"Hey, Justine," he called after me. "Maybe if I hung around you more, you'd be a good influence on me. I'm rapidly turning into a couch potato. You think you could get me into mountain biking?"

"I've . . . uh . . . given it up for the moment," I said.

"I can understand why," he said, still studying my leg. "But when your leg's healed, will you take me up on the trails with you?"

"So you can watch me in my next dramatic fall?"

"No, so you can turn me into an iron man!"

I still wasn't sure if he was teasing or not. I wasn't sure of anything with this guy. "If I decide to take it up again."

"Sure you will." He gave me an encouraging smile. "Tough girls like you who climb walls and rescue drowning kids don't let one little spill make you lose your nerve, right?"

"I guess not," I stammered. He was looking at me in a way that made me nervous. "I . . . uh . . . really should get Cassidy back inside and put these pants in the dryer."

He nodded. "And I really should get back to my

econ paper. Did you ever take an econ class?" He shuddered. "I don't recommend it."

"Carry me," Cassidy asked. I picked her up.

"Come on, let's go find you that cookie," I said. I was torn between wanting to go on talking to J.P. and wanting to get away from his teasing eyes.

I'd almost reached the back door when he called after me. "Hey, Justine. I'm meeting some friends tomorrow night. We'll probably go to Fiddler's Dream and just hang out. You want to come along? I'll pick you up."

"Okay," I managed to stammer.

"See ya, then." He smiled and waved as I closed the door behind me.

It wasn't until I had gotten Cassidy into dry clothes and thrown the wet stuff into the dryer that it hit me —I was going on a date with J.P.

My wildest dream was coming true!

# Chapter

# 10

"You're doing what?" Roni shrieked, loud enough for the entire hall to hear. It seemed like all three thousand students at Alta Mesa stood still waiting for my answer while I said, "I'm going on a date with J.P. tonight."

My friends were grinning as if they weren't sure whether to believe me or not.

"Right, Justine. In your dreams," Ginger said.

"You have the world's greatest imagination, Justine," Roni agreed. "You should write for the soaps."

"You're not serious, are you?" Karen asked. She was the only one who looked worried.

"I swear it. I am honestly, truly going on a date

with J.P. tonight and you guys have to help me figure out the right things to say. For example, just what is econ? What other subjects do you take in college? What's a good score on the SAT? And what are the names of some professors at ASU?"

"Justine!" Karen said in a horrified voice. "He doesn't really think that you're in college, does he?"

"He can't be that stupid," Ginger said scornfully. "Justine hardly looks like a college student."

"He thinks I'm the outdoor type," I said. "That explains why I'm so young and healthy looking."

"Justine, you're young and healthy looking because you're young and healthy!" Ginger cried. "I think *you're* forgetting that you're not in college!"

"You can't go out with a college guy," Roni said.

"Why not?"

"Because."

"Because why?"

"Because he's too old for you. Because college students drink and do all kinds of stuff that's too old for you."

"He's a nice guy! Besides, he only invited me to a coffeehouse, so there's nothing for you to worry about."

Roni rolled her eyes. "Bad things happen when

116

you pretend to be something you're not. This is just like that motorcycle guy."

"This is a coffeehouse, not a rock club," I snapped, "and J.P. is definitely not like Stryker. Stop trying to scare me!"

"Fine," Ginger said. "But don't say we didn't warn you."

All morning at school I swung between ecstasy and despair. I had a date with the guy of my dreams, but now that it was really about to happen, I wasn't sure I could handle it. Could I really bluff my way into a group of college students? What if they found out that I was a little high school freshman? I couldn't imagine anything worse. Somehow I had to be convincing without actually lying. I'd just have to keep steering the conversation to safer subjects. Then, when J.P. really liked me, I could tell him the truth . . . well, some of the truth. Maybe not the freshman part.

The thing that finally convinced me to go through with it was what happened in the cafeteria at lunchtime. We'd had a spring rainstorm overnight and the ground was still wet under our tree.

"When is it going to stop raining?" Ginger complained as we entered the cafeteria. We were met by a great blast of sound bouncing off the concrete walls.

"There's a table," Roni shouted. She started her typical crazy run toward it, but she stopped suddenly, knocking over someone's chair as she reached to steady herself. "Never mind," she said. "We don't want that one after all."

Of course, we all immediately looked at the table. I could see what Roni meant. Danny was at the next table with his friends.

"It's okay. I don't mind," I said, and I led the way to the table. "I'm completely over Danny." I hoped my voice would carry over all that noise. "Now that I've got J.P., I don't think I could ever look at a little freshman again."

I noticed with great satisfaction that Danny frowned. Great. So he *had* heard me. I grinned to myself and noticed that Michelle wasn't anywhere around. Maybe that relationship hadn't worked out after all. Maybe Danny was all alone, while I was about to be the new popular person in the college crowd. Revenge was sweet.

At least, it should have been sweet. Danny's friends got up and left the table. "See ya, Dan," one of them called. Danny stayed on, struggling with a humongous sandwich, the kind his mother always made him. He looked so lost sitting there by himself. I had a stupid urge to go sit with him, really close with our knees touching, the way we used to.

*Do I really want to go through with this?* I asked myself. *Am I really ready to get involved with a college guy?* I glanced over and met Danny's gaze.

"Hi, Justine. How's it going?" he called.

"Great," I said. "How about you?"

He shrugged. "Oh, pretty good. Busy these days?"

"Crazy," I shouted back. "With my afternoon job and—"

I didn't get to finish my sentence because a shape loomed up behind Danny. It was Michelle, in black jeans and a tight T-shirt. "Hi, gorgeous," she cooed. "Sorry I'm late. Were you lonesome without me?" She slid into the seat beside him. "It was sweet of you to wait."

*He was just trying to finish that sandwich,* I wanted to say. *And he was talking to me.* But I didn't.

"Sorry, Jus, what were you saying?" Danny called, giving me an embarrassed grin as Michelle moved in so close that she was almost eating Danny's sandwich.

"I just said that I had this crazy schedule and

then major weekend plans," I said. "Big date to-night."

"Great. Good for you," he said halfheartedly. I turned back to my friends and didn't look at him once during the rest of the meal.

Now I had to go through with the date. I tried not to worry about it too much, because I always say dumb things when I'm nervous. I had to stay cool no matter what. Normally before a date I'd spend all afternoon getting ready, but today I had a two-year-old terror waiting for me.

"Hi, Justine!" Cassidy called from the gate at the top of the stairs.

Mrs. Holmes beamed at me. "She likes you already. And you've done wonders with her, Justine. Just between you and me, we were getting worried about her hostile behavior to the baby. My husband was ready to take her to our psychiatrist."

"It's perfectly normal for an only child to resent a new baby," I said. "Trust me."

She patted my hand. "I'm glad we found you, Justine. I have to admit, I was a little worried that you weren't a college student yet, but you seem to be just what Cassidy needs."

I bit my lip. "Well, actually, I'm not even a senior in high school yet," I blurted. "I should have told you before, but I was afraid you wouldn't hire me."

Mrs. Holmes smiled. "I know you aren't a senior," she said. "But you're a very mature young woman and we're delighted to have you."

I went upstairs in a blaze of glory, glad that she hadn't seen me trying to climb her ivy on the first day. But inside I was glowing. I was actually good at this job. I'd done something right! It felt great.

I was so busy all afternoon that I completely forgot about my date until I got on my bike to ride home. As I pulled out of the driveway, J.P. called to me from his yard. He asked for my address, so he'd know where to pick me up tonight. I think I managed to keep my voice steady while I talked to him, but I had to concentrate really hard to ride home safely. My head was spinning, and all my nagging doubts had come back.

"You can handle this," I said out loud to myself. "Mrs. Holmes even told you that you were mature. So relax. It's going to be great."

I kept up that positive attitude until Karen called me around seven. "I really don't think you should do this, Justine," she said.

"You make it sound like I'm joining a terrorist group," I said, attempting a casual laugh.

121

"You know what I mean," she said. "College students are too old for you."

"Karen," I said, "just remember that I've led a more sophisticated life than you—"

"That's what I mean," Karen interrupted. "Watch what you say tonight. You know you tend to boast sometimes . . ."

I started to say "I do not," but then I shut up. I have been known, occasionally, to tell my friends about my trips to Europe and my romantic adventures with foreign men. I guess that might have made them jealous.

"I'll be careful, okay?" I said. "I won't say a word all night. I'll just sit there smiling like the Mona Lisa. Now are you satisfied?"

I shook my head as Karen hung up. Why did my friends have to be so worried about me? It made me nervous. I went straight to my closet. Thinking about clothes always calms me down.

I'd have liked to wear my black miniskirt and black halter top. They certainly don't make me look like a freshman. But I didn't want to show my scarred leg to the world, so I had to put on a pair of the silky pants that Christine had bought me. I chose the black-and-brown African print pants and I did wear the halter top. That's about the sexiest thing I own.

122

"You look good," Christine commented as I came downstairs. "Very grown up."

I beamed.

"I just hope your father's not too late tonight," she said, looking anxiously at the clock. "And I hope he comes home with good news. He should know today whether he has to go to London or not."

"Why can't he find someone to go for him?" I demanded.

"I think it's a really big crisis," she said. "He has to handle it himself. But why did it have to blow up right now, just when the baby is due?"

"Don't worry," I said soothingly. "First babies are always late, aren't they? Even if he has to go to London, he'll be back by the time anything happens."

"I hope so." She frowned. "This baby stuff is scary when you haven't done it before."

"Hey, I'm the expert now," I said. "I've even changed diapers."

She made a face. "It's not the diaper part I'm worried about—it's the delivery part. I'd just hate it if your father wasn't there."

"He will be," I assured her.

I felt kind of bad about leaving her when J.P.'s horn sounded. In many ways Christine was okay—

better than other mothers, in fact. She hadn't even quizzed me about going out tonight. I'd told her I was going to a coffeehouse with some friends, and she had just assumed they were friends from school. She'd even been relieved that one of them was giving me a ride. All she'd said was "Don't be late," and I'd agreed. I wondered how she'd act if she knew that the friend who was picking me up was really a hunky college man.

I didn't know how to act myself. Taking a deep breath, I headed out on my first date with an older guy.

# 11

I ran outside, and there was J.P., stepping like Prince Charming from his yellow Porsche. Tonight he was wearing a black ASU Sun Devils T-shirt over black casual pants and he looked even more gorgeous than I'd remembered. He seemed to approve of the way I looked too.

"No concealed weapons tonight," I attempted to joke, because the way he was looking at me was making me nervous.

"I don't know about that," he said as he closed the car door behind me.

I wasn't quite sure what he meant by that remark, so I asked quickly, "You want to put on some music?"

"Sure. What do you like?"

"Anything. Whatever you like."

"There should be some Stones lying around on the floor."

"Excuse me?" I thought I hadn't heard right. What did stones on the floor have to do with music?

"A Stones CD, by your feet somewhere."

I reached down and picked up a CD titled *The Rolling Stones in Concert.* I felt myself blushing. I hadn't even thought of the *Rolling* Stones. Boy, was I glad I hadn't put my foot in my mouth big time.

"I'm really into classic stuff," he said. "The Who. The Stones. How about you?"

"Oh, sure," I said. All I knew about the Stones was that they were a bunch of old guys that my dad and Christine listened to. But I put the CD into the player. He even had a CD player in his car! This guy was mega-cool. The music was great. The beat vibrated through the tiny cabin of the Porsche and made talking almost impossible. We were both singing along to old Mick Jagger songs by the time we pulled up at the parking lot behind the coffeehouse.

Tempe was loud and lively as we stepped out into the warm night. Where I live, everything closes up by eight, but the streets here were full, with music spilling from almost every doorway. A girl was standing on the sidewalk playing a flute, and groups of students sat outside, drinking coffee. It all looked very different and exciting, even to a girl who's been to Paris.

J.P. ushered me into the dark coffeehouse. "There are the guys," he said, gesturing to a booth at the back. He said "guys," but actually there were equal numbers of girls and guys around the table. All of them were long haired and way older than me. They all looked at me with interest.

"Hey, everyone, this is Justine. I told you about her," J.P. announced.

"The lady triathlete?" the boy nearest me asked as I squeezed myself in beside him.

"Mountain biker," J.P. corrected.

"Oh, right. You broke your leg mountain biking," one of the girls said with a smile that didn't look altogether friendly.

"Only grazed it," I said. "It just looks gross."

I wished instantly that I hadn't used that word. *Gross* sounded so juvenile.

"Where do you go mountain biking?" asked a guy at the far end of the table. "I haven't seen any good trails around here yet. I want to bring my bike down from California next semester."

Again everyone was looking at me. "Oh, there are good trails," I said, hoping that the light was dim enough to hide my pink cheeks. "You just have to go out a ways first. Up in the mountains, you know."

"Well, otherwise they wouldn't call them mountain bikes, would they?" the girl with the creepy smile said.

I smiled back at her.

"I know you from somewhere," another girl commented. "Are you in my English class?"

"I—I'm not sure," I stammered, praying that classes at ASU were so large that nobody would notice if I was there or not.

"You'd know if you were," she said. "We are definitely suffering with James Joyce."

"Is he in the class too?" I asked.

They all burst out laughing.

I wasn't sure what I'd said that was funny, but I was definitely not going to let them go on asking me about classes.

"See, I told you she had a great sense of humor," J.P. said, and gave me a wink that made me feel like I was melting inside.

"So, Justine, you're looking after Superbrat next door to J.P., right?" the guy next to me asked.

I nodded.

128

"Mrs. Holmes called me to see if I'd do it," one of the girls said, "but I told her I didn't have time with finals coming up. How on earth do you manage it, Justine?"

"It's only afternoons." I shrugged.

"I was glad I had an excuse," she went on. "From what J.P.'s been telling us, the kid is a monster."

"She's not that bad," I said.

"Apart from throwing herself and her toys into the pool and hiding the baby and locking you out, it's been an uneventful week, right, Justine?" J.P. asked, his eyes holding mine again.

"And I bet you just had to check on her to see if she needed any help," the creepy girl said.

"You know me, always ready to lend a hand," J.P. answered. He didn't look at her.

I sensed strange vibes going between them. I got the feeling that maybe she was an old girlfriend who was jealous that he'd brought me. I grinned to myself at the thought of a college woman being jealous of me.

The waiter arrived to take our order. I said "Cappuccino," which was the only fancy coffee name I could remember.

"Isn't this place great?" I said to the guy next to me. And it *was* great! People were playing chess, listening to music. How different from the juvenile little pizza parlors where we high school kids hung out.

The guy looked at me in surprise. "Is this the first time you've been here?"

It was too late to back down. I nodded.

"Where do you usually hang out?"

"Friends' houses," I said, feeling stupid again. "This place is like the coffeehouses I used to go to in Europe."

Finally I'd said something right. They were all instantly interested. "You were in Europe? Did you study over there?"

"No, just vacation."

"Where?"

"All over, really. I've been there several times."

"Wow, I'm jealous. I'm dying to go when I can get the money together. Did you stay in youth hostels?"

"Sometimes." I didn't want to admit that I'd always stayed in hotels with my dad.

"Have you been to Paris? I'm dying to go to Paris," a serious girl with long black hair asked.

Luckily I knew Paris well. Suddenly I was the center of attention, telling them about food and French waiters and romantic strolls along the

Seine. And if I stretched the truth just a little when I talked about my adventures on the Left Bank, I'm sure anyone would have done the same.

I spent the drive home in a bright bubble of happiness. I'd faced the test and I'd passed. Those ASU students actually liked me! They thought I was interesting. They were impressed with my travels. I was a success.

"So what are we doing tomorrow night?" one of the girls had asked as the coffeehouse announced it was closing.

"We could meet somewhere and decide then," J.P. said. He looked right at me. "I feel like a really great party. Let's see whose party we're going to crash. Okay?" The okay was directed to me, too.

The music was loud again on the way home. I sat very close to J.P. Every now and then he'd turn and give me a little questioning smile.

"You want to go for a drive somewhere?" he asked me as we got close to my house.

"My stepmother's home alone. I should probably go back," I said. "She's very nervous right now."

He shrugged. "Okay. Whatever you want." He pulled over to the curb. "Can I pick you up the same time tomorrow?"

"Sure," I said. "Thanks very much for asking

me, J.P. I had a great time. I really like your friends."

"What about me?" he asked. His eyes were bright in the glow of the streetlamp.

"I really like you too," I whispered.

He laughed, then he took the back of my head in his hands, pulled me toward him, and kissed me. I had always thought that Danny was a good kisser. His kisses had made me feel all tingly and warm. But J.P.'s kiss was nothing like that. It was so intense and demanding that it took my breath away and made me realize that Danny had been a complete beginner.

But incredible as it made me feel, I found myself wondering whether I really was letting myself in for more than I could handle.

# 12

As I confessed before, I have been known to stretch the truth sometimes. All that stuff about me and the cute guys from the boys' prep school when I was at Sagebrush, and the French waiters on the Champs Elysées—it didn't actually happen the way I told them. I know I seem like the kind of girl who has incredible romances all over the world, but the truth is that Danny was my first real boyfriend. Inside this beautiful, smooth exterior, I'm really kind of shy. Okay, so now I've said it.

But when Roni called me for details the next morning, for once I didn't have to brag or exaggerate.

"So how was your date?" she yelled into the phone.

"Talk loud. Ginger's here and she's listening too."

Suddenly I felt weird. For the first time in my life I really did have something to brag about. I had kissed a college guy in his Porsche. But I found that I didn't want to brag about it. If I told them how J.P. had kissed me, they'd probably never believe me anyway.

"It was great," I said. "We went to a coffeehouse and just hung out with his friends."

"And nobody guessed that you were only a high school freshman?"

"Not at all," I said. "We got to talking about Europe and, as you know, I am an expert when it comes to Europe."

"Justine, you're something else." Roni chuckled. "So you and this J.P. guy really hit it off?"

"I'm seeing him again tonight," I said.

"No kidding? Where are you going?"

"We haven't decided yet, but somewhere fun."

"Wow, Justine. I'm impressed," Roni said. There was mumbling in the background. "Ginger is impressed too," Roni reported, "but she says to be careful and not get carried away. Remember, he really is too old for you, Justine."

"He's also a perfect gentleman," I said. "He kissed me good night in the car."

"He did? How was it?"

"Like wow," I said.

There was a pause. "Justine, you'd better be careful," Roni said slowly.

"Stop worrying!" I told her. "You sound like Karen."

"Okay," Roni said doubtfully. "I guess you know what you're doing. So we won't see you at the sleepover tonight?"

"I guess not. Say hi to Ginger and Karen for me."

"Sure will. I'm not sure whether to say have fun or take care."

"How about both?" I said, laughing.

"Okay, both."

I was smiling as I hung up. I had done something none of my friends had ever done, and they were impressed. Now I knew kids—or rather, young adults—in college! Maybe they'd get to be my friends too. Of course, that would mean I'd have to learn to ride a mountain bike in the near future, or I'd look like a phony. But I couldn't worry about that today. Tonight I was meeting the new love of my life, and it was going to be even more fun than last night.

I went down to my dad's study and got out the encyclopedia, flipping through it to read up on the sort of things college students probably knew. Econ—that was way too complicated to read in a hurry. Sigmund Freud—I should probably know about him, I decided. I was engrossed in all the various psychological terms when my dad strode into the room, followed by Christine.

"It can't be helped," he was saying.

"It *could* be helped if you cared about me more than your job." Christine was in tears.

Neither of them saw me until Dad almost stepped on me.

"Justine," he said. "What are you doing here?"

"Reading up on Sigmund Freud."

"Could you take the book somewhere else, please?" he said. "I have to get my things together. I've got to leave for London in an hour."

"You're really going to London?" I asked. "What about Christine and the baby?"

"I don't want to go, Justine," he said, "but it seems as if I'm the only one who can sort things out over there. I'll be back by the baby's due date, I promise."

"What if it's early?" Christine demanded.

"First babies are always late. Trust me. Justine was a whole week late," Dad said. "Please don't worry, honeybun. I'll be here. I promise."

"I'm glad Justine is here," Christine said. "She's a big comfort to me."

"Sure she is," Dad said in the hearty voice he uses when he's not quite sure of himself. "Take good care of her, Justine. Make sure she has nothing to worry about."

"We'll be fine, Dad," I told him. "Say hi to London for me."

The limo came for him soon after. Christine was really upset. She stood at the window and watched him go, still crying. I don't know why she felt like that. If I was having a baby, the last person I'd want around would be my dad. He's clumsy and he gets embarrassed so easily. I bet he'd get in the way in the delivery room, or even faint. But I decided not to say any of this to Christine. She wanted him there, so that was what mattered.

It was only when I started to get ready that it occurred to me she might not want to be left alone tonight. I breezed down to the living room.

"You'll be okay if I go out with my friends for a while, won't you?" I asked. "I decided not to sleep over at Roni's house tonight."

Good tactics. She smiled at me gratefully. "How thoughtful of you, Justine. No, please, go out with your friends. There's no reason why you should sit

137

around with me all evening. I'll just watch an old movie on TV and then go to bed early."

"Good idea," I said. She wouldn't even be awake when I got home. That would prevent having to admit to embarrassing things like curfews. I was tempted to ask if I could go through her wardrobe to see if she had anything that would make me look like a college student, but I decided not to push my luck. After all, I do have more clothes than anyone I know, so wanting an outfit I didn't own might make her suspicious.

In the end I settled for the other pair of the silky pants Christine had bought me. They were a soft gray and I owned a gray silk shirt, which I tied above the waist. Not bad at all! The gray was really flattering with my blond hair and tan. *Gray is such a mature color,* I thought happily. All I needed was a mature hairstyle and I'd be set. With the help of zillions of bobby pins I got my hair to stay back in a sophisticated French knot. I even gooped all the flyaway strands so that every hair was in place. Now I really looked grown up. I added red lipstick, eyeliner, and lots of mascara. *Am I gorgeous or what?* I thought.

J.P.'s eyes lit up when he saw me. "Wow," he said. "I'm glad you threw out your 'save the world' image tonight, because we're going to start off somewhere fancy."

I noticed he was wearing a sport jacket and gray slacks. He looked like a man in them. He wasn't playing at being grown up, like me. He *was* grown up. I felt a jolt of fear, until he took my chin in his fingers and gave me the gentlest of kisses. "Hi," he whispered.

We drove together through dark deserted streets until I noticed that the neighborhood seemed familiar.

"Where are we going?" I asked, horrified. But I already knew the answer. We swung in through impressive wrought-iron gates. The sign over them said MOUNTAIN SHADOWS COUNTRY CLUB.

*My* country club. The club where my dad hung out all the time and where I had competed in the junior golf tournament.

"Uh . . . what are we doing here?" My voice came out high and weird.

"Moonlight golf?" J.P. suggested. Then he laughed. "There's a reception here for the ASU golf team. Glen and Doug were on the team and I subbed a couple of times, so we thought we'd meet here. You know what guys who live in dorms are like. They never say no to free food."

My mind was racing. Someone at the country club was sure to recognize me. They'd say something embarrassing like "Hi, Justine. How's high school going?"

My only chance was to get us out of there as quickly as possible. My legs were actually shaking as I got out of the car. I walked beside J.P. up the familiar flight of steps and into the foyer. Music and laughter floated out from the reception room on our right. A couple of old guys were leaving the bar. They seemed to recognize me, and nodded as I went past. *They should have known who I am,* I thought. *Dad plays golf with them all the time.* Maybe my disguise was good enough. Maybe I really did look like a different, older person. Was it possible that I'd get away with it?

The lights were dimmed in the reception room, with candles at the tables and a DJ playing music at one end. J.P. took my hand to lead me through the crowd. His friends were around the punch bowl. One of them handed me a glass of punch.

"Hi, Justine. Sorry. Only nonalcoholic. They're making us show ID if we want a beer."

"That's what I call mean-spirited," J.P. said. "A party with no beer? I don't think we'll be staying long."

"That's okay, because Patrick's having a kegger at his place."

140

"Patrick's place?" J.P. asked. "You mean his cabin?"

"Sure. His folks are in New York and the place was empty, so we thought, why not?"

"Why not?" J.P. laughed. He gave me a questioning look. I wasn't sure what the answer was because I hadn't understood the question. So I sipped my punch and hoped I was invisible. All I knew was that I definitely didn't like the sound of a kegger at a cabin. I'd fantasized about going to grown-up parties, but now I wasn't so sure.

I moved across to one of the hors d'oeuvres tables and started to help myself to mini-quiches and raw veggies. I dipped a carrot into the spinach dip and had just taken a big bite when I heard a voice behind me.

"No meatballs. I hate it when they go all health-conscious."

I almost choked on my carrot. I spun around and found myself a foot away from Danny. I don't know which of us was more startled.

I recovered first. "Danny, hi. What a surprise."

"Justine?" he croaked. "What are you doing here?"

"I'm here with my date," I said. "He's on the ASU golf team and it's their reception. How about you?"

"My dad's one of the sponsors," he said.

I thought of saying something crushing about being sponsored by a garbage company, but I didn't. I'd show him who was classy.

"That's nice," I said. "Did you bring Michelle?"

"She . . . uh . . . went to the powder room," he said.

"Are things still good with you two?"

"Oh, yeah, just great," he said. "What's this about you and a guy from ASU?"

"That's right. Oh, do me a favor, Danny. If you meet him, don't mention anything about me being a freshman in high school. I didn't tell him."

"Jus, are you crazy?" he cried.

"I know what I'm doing," I snapped, annoyed by his concerned look.

"Okay, okay," he said. He kept staring at me. Finally he said, "You look great, Justine. So grown up. I hardly know you."

"Well, girls mature faster than boys, remember." I gave him my sweetest smile. He did look kind of adorable, in a little-boy way.

Suddenly Michelle was at his elbow, and he didn't look so cute anymore. "Sorry I was gone so long, babe," she cooed. Then she did a double take when she saw me. It was very satisfying. "I see you've found someone to keep you busy." Then she slipped her arm through his, giving me a look that said very clearly, "Stay away from my guy."

"I really have to go," I said. "We only just stopped by here for a few minutes. We're on our way to a party up at a friend's cabin."

I saw J.P. scanning the room, looking for me. I grabbed a mini-quiche as I made my way back to him, very conscious of Danny's and Michelle's eyes following me.

"Hi," I whispered. "Did you miss me? I brought you some food." Then I popped the mini-quiche into his mouth.

"They must have known you were coming, Justine." J.P. chuckled. "All the food is healthy and environmentally correct. Personally I'd have gone for ribs and hot dogs."

He turned back to his friend Doug. "How about we take some stuff to barbecue up to the cabin with us?"

"I think Patrick already did."

"Then what are we waiting for?" J.P. asked. "I've put in my appearance here, so we can split." He looked at me. "If you want to, that is."

Danny was still hovering nearby, so I talked extra loud. "Sure," I said, taking J.P.'s hand. "There is absolutely nothing to keep me here."

"Kegger, here we come!" Doug shouted.

J.P. swung around. "Be quiet, stupid! Do you want the world to know where we're going?"

"Sorry," Doug said, not sounding sorry at all. "Do you know how to get there?"

"Better write me out directions again," J.P. said. "Justine can navigate for me. She's a pro when it comes to mountain trails, remember."

A jolt of alarm went through me. Mountain trails?

"Just how far away is this place?" I asked lightly.

"It's doable," he said with an easy smile. "About an hour's drive, out past Prescott."

"That far, huh?"

"You don't want to go?"

"I'm, uh, not really dressed for mountain cabins."

"We don't have to go if you don't want to."

Danny had moved nearer. I could feel, rather than see, him hovering behind me. "Don't be silly." I laughed. "I'd love to come. It sounds like a blast."

"Okay, these are the directions. Pay attention," Doug said, waving a piece of paper at J.P.

My arm was grabbed from behind and Danny swung me around. "You can't be serious," he hissed. "You're not going to a cabin in the mountains with that guy!"

"Why not?"

He glared at me. "Because he's too old for you and I don't want you in a cabin with a group of drunk guys."

"What do you care?" I demanded.

"I care enough not to want you to do something dumb," he said.

"I think you're just jealous that I've found somebody better than you," I said. "Why don't you go back to Michelle? You'll only get in trouble with her if you stay here talking to me."

I started to turn away, but he took my hand. "Jus, please don't do this," he said.

His eyes bored into mine, and I couldn't look away. If he'd said, "Stay here with me. Forget about this J.P. guy. He doesn't love you the way I do," then I'm sure I would have stayed.

But Michelle's high voice cut across the room. "Danny! This is my favorite song. Come dance with me."

"You'd better go," I said. "You're being called."

J.P. came up beside me and wrapped a big arm around my shoulders. "Are you ready to split?" he asked, smiling down at me.

"Sure," I said.

I walked out without looking back.

# 13

The night was very dark. Our headlights were narrow beams of brightness that swung crazily around as we took the bends at high speed. J.P. had his foot down and the Porsche was showing just how fast it could go on a deserted road.

Ever since we had left the country club, the scared feeling had been growing inside me. I wondered what could have gotten into my head to make me agree to go up to the mountains with a guy I hardly knew. Actually, when I thought about it, I knew exactly what had gotten into my head. Danny. I'd wanted to shock him and impress him and make him die with jealousy. But the farther we drove from the bright lights of

Phoenix, the more I realized just how dumb I had been.

*It's only a party,* I kept telling myself. *J.P.'s a nice guy. His friends are all nice. I can handle it. It might even be fun.* And my friends would be blown away when I told them I had spent the night in the mountains at a wild party. Roni's eyes would pop out of her head!

But these thoughts only made me more frightened. The words "spending the night" spun around in my head. We weren't really going to stay up at the cabin all night, were we? I thought about Christine in the house alone. She'd said she was going to go to bed early, but what if she couldn't sleep? What if she got up at one or two and found that I wasn't back? Maybe I could call and tell her that I'd decided to spend the night at Roni's after all.

"Is there a phone at the cabin?" I asked casually.

J.P. shrugged. "I don't know. It's pretty primitive out there. Why?"

"My stepmother's in the house alone," I said. "I should check in with her so that she doesn't worry."

J.P. grinned. "Still keeping tabs on you, huh? That's one of the real downers of living at home. They still treat you like a little kid. My folks are fine

148

most of the time, but when I come in at four in the morning, you'd think I was fourteen years old by the way they carry on. That's why I'm planning to get my own place next semester. How about you? Are you going to move out?"

"I'm not sure," I said cautiously.

J.P. swung the car abruptly to the right and I felt the tires skid on gravel.

"What's wrong?" I asked.

"Great view from here," he said. He inched the car forward until there was a gap between hills. Suddenly the whole city was below us, sparkling in the clear night air.

"It's very pretty," I said.

"So are you," he murmured. Then he put his hands around my head and drew me close to him. The kiss was a repeat of last night's, only better—and more scary. I was feeling things I'd never felt before, but at the same time alarm bells were going off in my head. This would soon be something I couldn't control—something I might not even *want* to control.

"Just wait until we get to that cozy cabin, huh?" J.P. whispered in my ear.

I took a deep breath, like a diver coming up for air. The breath turned into a sob, a huge, gut-wrenching sob that surprised even me. J.P. looked at me in alarm. "What's wrong?"

"Everything," I said, trying to get the word out before I started crying.

"You don't want to go to the cabin?"

I shook my head, because I was scared that if I opened my mouth, I'd bawl like a baby.

"What's with you?" he demanded. "You were the one who couldn't wait to get out of the country club! You were flirting with me like crazy, but now suddenly you act like I'm turning you off."

"It's not that." I sniffled.

"You don't like me? You didn't like it when I kissed you?"

I took a deep breath and fought down my panic. "That's the problem. I liked it too much. It made me feel—" I broke off, because I couldn't find the word.

J.P. laughed uneasily. "Well, what's the problem? I like you, you like me, and we're going to have a great time together. What's wrong with that?"

I had no choice. "You don't understand," I said. "I've been lying to you all week. Well, not lying, actually, but I didn't correct you when you thought that I was something I wasn't. . . ."

"Excuse me?" he said. "What are you trying to

say? That you're really a man in disguise? A creature from outer space?"

"No," I said. "I'm trying to say that I don't go to ASU."

"So?" He was still smiling. "That's not the biggest crime in the world. Not everybody has to go to college."

"I don't go because I'm only fifteen," I said in a rush. "I'm a freshman in high school."

He shrank back as if I'd just told him I had leprosy. "You're what?"

"I'm a freshman at Alta Mesa," I said.

"Why didn't you tell me earlier?"

I stared out of the window at the grids of light below us. "Because you thought I was an ASU student and I knew you'd never be interested in me if you knew how old I was."

I turned to look back at him, willing him to understand.

"Boy, you sure live dangerously for a fifteen-year-old," he said. "Going to a cabin with a bunch of people you don't know. Do you make a habit of this?"

"No!" I said in horror.

"Didn't it occur to you that you might be asking for trouble, driving up to the mountains with a college guy?"

"Only now," I said. "It just occurred to me now."

"And what about getting back? Did you think about that? What if I refuse to drive you back and just dump you here? It's a long dark walk, Justine. Had that occurred to you?"

I shook my head, staring at him with big, scared eyes.

He snorted. "Boy, you really must be naive."

I opened my mouth to say that I wasn't at all naive. I was a sophisticated world traveler. But I swallowed back the words before they could escape. "I am naive," I said. "And pretty dumb too, I guess."

I saw his face soften. "Not completely dumb," he said. "You have good taste. I'm a nice guy. You're safe with me. I'll drive you home now."

"But you'll miss your party," I said softly.

"I can drive up later if I feel like it," he said. "The most important thing is getting you home."

"Thanks, J.P.," I said. "You really are a nice guy. I wish I were five years older."

He gave me a gentle look. "I wish you were too," he said.

He started the car and we took off again, tires screeching on the gravel as he swung the car back toward the city. We were down among the bright lights again in only half an hour. I was surprised to see that it was just ten o'clock as we headed for my house. I felt as if I'd been away for half a lifetime.

"Thanks again, J.P.," I said as we drew up outside my front gate. "You really are the world's sweetest guy. I'm sorry I lied to you. It was just that . . . you seemed like my dream guy, the guy I'd always wanted to meet."

He reached out and stroked my cheek. "You'll meet your dream guy someday, Justine. Hey, maybe I'll stick around. When you're done with college— let's say you're twenty-one and I'm twenty-six, who knows?" And he gave me a wonderful smile.

"One more thing, Justine," he said as I went to open the car door.

"What?"

"Don't ever try a stunt like this again, you hear me? If I were your parents I'd ground you until you *were* twenty-one, just to be on the safe side."

I laughed. "Don't worry. I've learned my lesson. From now on I just hang out with kids my own age."

"That's my girl," he said, and the way he said it made me feel warm inside. He reached across to open my door for me. "See you next time you have a crisis with the Holmes kids," he said.

"Okay. Bye, J.P."

"Bye, Justine."

I waved as he drove away. He really was the world's sweetest guy. Why did he have to be too old for me? Did he really mean that about getting together when I was through with college? If so, it was something worth waiting for, worth dreaming about. I pictured myself returning from studying in Paris, full of European flair, and meeting J.P. at the country club. "Justine," he'd say. "I can't believe it. You've grown into a beautiful woman."

I smiled to myself as I waltzed down the front path, wrapped in my beautiful fantasy. I was a couple of steps from the front door when a dark shape suddenly loomed up in front of me. My heart flip-flopped. I opened my mouth to scream, but no sound would come. I couldn't decide whether to try to make it to the front door or to run back the way I had come.

"Keep away from me," I whimpered.

But the dark shape kept on coming.

# Chapter

## 14

"Justine, it's me," said a familiar voice.

"Danny?" I gasped. "You scared the daylights out of me. What on earth are you doing here?"

"I'm sorry. I didn't mean to scare you."

"But what are you doing here?"

"I was worried about you," he said. "I didn't like the thought of you going up to a kegger party with a bunch of wild guys. I would have gone after you if I'd been able to drive. I decided the next-best thing was to tell your folks."

"You told Christine?" Shivers were going down my spine. I really was going to be grounded until I was twenty-one.

He shook his head. "I couldn't. There's nobody

home. That's why I was sitting here. I decided to wait for them to get back."

"Nobody home?" I repeated. "Christine said she was going to bed early. I can't imagine her going out in her shape. Maybe she's asleep."

I got out my key and opened the front door. The first thing I saw was a note on the hall table:

*Justine, I think this is it. I've gone to the hospital. Please tell your father if he calls. I'm not too thrilled about doing this alone.*

I looked at the note and then at Danny.

"Bad news?" he asked.

"My stepmother. She's gone to the hospital to have the baby, and I wasn't here. Oh, Danny, I feel terrible! She's at the hospital all by herself."

"What about your dad?"

"He had to fly to London today. The baby isn't due for another week. I hope everything's okay. They've been so excited about this baby . . . I just hope . . . Danny, I've got to get to the hospital right now!"

"I'd drive you if I had my license." He paused, then added, "Maybe you shouldn't have sent the guy in the Porsche away. He could have driven you." He sounded a little bit jealous, I thought.

"Yeah, well, it's too late for that now," I said. "I have to get there somehow."

"Call a taxi," he said.

"Danny, you're brilliant! Why didn't I think of that? Get the yellow pages. Taxi . . ." I could barely think straight, and I even had a hard time looking up the listing. "Will you call for me?" I asked him. "My hands are shaking so much, I don't think I can hold the phone."

"Relax," he said, patting my arm. "It's going to be okay."

"I hope so," I said. "It's early, Danny. Is that all right? I feel so guilty about not being here."

"It could have happened anytime, Justine. It could have been while you were in school. I'm sure your stepmother didn't expect you to sit home just in case."

"I know, but . . ."

Danny was dialing, then ordering the taxi in a calm, strong voice. He put down the phone again. "They say about ten minutes," he said. Then he cleared his throat. "Is that why you came back early? Because you felt guilty about leaving your stepmother?"

"That and other things," I said. I went over and sat on the bottom step of the staircase, hugging my knees to stop the shaking.

He came to sit beside me. "Things like what?"

When I didn't say anything he added, "Did that college guy come on strong? Did he turn out to be a jerk?"

I shook my head. "It wasn't him. It was me," I said. "I couldn't go through with it. I think I knew all along that I was getting myself into something that was way over my head. And the farther we got from the city, the more scared I was." I didn't add that the way J.P. was kissing me also had something to do with it.

"So you never got to the cabin?"

I shook my head again. "I made J.P. drive me home."

Danny chuckled. "I bet he was pleased about that," he said. "What excuse did you give?"

"I told him the truth," I said.

He looked surprised. "Good for you."

"It wasn't good for me," I said. "It was doing what I should have done right away. He thought I was a college student and I let him think it. I guess I was flattered that a great-looking college guy was paying attention to me."

He nodded. "I can understand that. I'd be flattered if a college girl started hanging around me." Then a big grin crossed his face. "Scared silly, but flattered."

I had to laugh. "Danny, I'm so glad you're here. I

still can't believe you wrecked your own Saturday night because you were worried about me."

"Someone had to," he said. "I imagined you up there with all those drunk college guys, and I got so angry I was ready to climb on my bike and go after them."

I smiled at the image of Danny puffing away on his ten-speed behind J.P.'s Porsche. "I don't know what to say, Danny. I've never had anyone care about me like that before. But what did you tell Michelle? Wasn't she mad?"

He nodded. "Furious. In fact, she had a temper tantrum, right there at the country club."

"How embarrassing."

"It was. But I guess I should have expected it. She always gets mad when she can't get her own way. She's spoiled rotten—even worse than you."

"Gee, thanks a lot."

"Actually, you're not spoiled at all, compared to Michelle," he said. "You've turned out okay, considering that you're an only child with all that money."

"But not too much attention," I reminded him. "Maybe that was what saved me, even though I'd rather have love than money." Danny nodded. "So why do you stay with Michelle if she's such a brat?" I asked.

"I don't," he said. "I told her tonight that enough was enough." He spread his hands and looked down at them. "I was like you, I guess—flattered that a popular cheerleader was hanging around me. And also it was a great excuse to get out of—"

He paused, embarrassed.

"You wanted to get out of going steady with me?"

"Uh-huh. But don't get me wrong, Justine. It has nothing to do with you. I still care about you, as you can see. I was beginning to feel trapped. My friends were teasing me with all these dumb jokes about when I was going to buy the ring . . . I just got scared."

"I know how you feel," I said. "High school should be a time for dating lots of different people and just having fun."

"Yeah," he said. "Don't tell me you felt the same way?"

"It was going through my mind," I confessed.

"That's so weird," he said. "And we never talked about it."

"Because we didn't want to hurt each other."

He nodded. "You'll always be special to me, Justine. My first girlfriend."

"Same goes for me, Danny."

"You don't want to get back together again, do you?"

160

I was tempted. Boy, was I tempted. Danny was sitting close beside me, and I could feel his warmth and smell his cologne. But I was still trying to be mature, and to think about what was best for both of us.

"Let's just stay friends for now," I said. "Being tied to one person when you're only fifteen isn't very smart. We need to refine our flirting skills."

He laughed. "I'd say yours were already pretty good, judging from the way you were carrying on with that college jerk."

"Yours weren't too bad either, the way you were carrying on with the whole cafeteria watching at school."

Danny blushed. "We can still go out together sometimes, right?" he asked. "To a movie or for a pizza, just as friends?"

"I'd like that, Danny."

"Me too."

There was the sound of a car drawing up outside.

"The taxi's here," I said, getting up. "I wonder if there's anything Christine needs me to take for her. I hope they won't make me stay with her in the delivery room. I don't know if I could handle that . . . ohmygosh, these clothes aren't right for a hospital,

161

are they?" I couldn't even think straight, I was so worried about Christine.

Danny grabbed my shoulders. "Justine?" he said simply. "Would you like me to come with you?"

"To the hospital?"

He nodded. "I could call my folks and explain. I'm sure it would be okay."

I'd never been more relieved in my life. "Oh, Danny, I'd love that. I'm so scared, my legs are like jelly."

"No problem," he said. "Go tell the taxi to wait while I call home. And you'd better grab a jacket, too. It might be a long night."

He gave me a wonderful, comforting smile—the smile of a good friend. I smiled back as I ran out to the taxi.

# Chapter

# 15

The next moments were unreal—the dark, empty streets, the crackle of the taxi's radio, the brightly lit admitting area of the hospital, the smell of disinfectant, the disembodied voices calling for doctors, flashing lights, speeding gurneys . . . everything was so different from my normal life. I felt as if I was dreaming as I took the elevator up to the fifth floor. I was so glad that Danny was beside me. He was my one point of reality in this whole bizarre world.

Up on the maternity floor, the nurse made Danny go to the waiting area, then showed me into a dimly lit room. I don't know what I expected to see—something out of *ER*, maybe, with a huge medical team and lots of panic. Instead it looked like a hotel room, with prints on the wall and soft pastel bedclothes. Christine was lying in bed watching TV. She looked up when I came in, and a big smile spread over her face.

"Justine! You found me! How did you get here?"

"Taxi," I said. "Danny came with me. He's waiting outside."

"I'm so glad you came," she said, reaching out her hand to me. "It's lonely in here."

"I bet," I said. "This is a weird place. So what's happening? Is the baby really coming?"

"They said sometime tonight," she said. "Right now I'm pretty comfortable. I'm just getting contractions every five minutes or so. And the breathing I've practiced is working pretty well so far. But I wish your father was here. He was supposed to coach me. We went to all the classes together. . . ."

"It's just like Dad," I said. "He was never there for any of my dance recitals or tennis games at school. He always promised he'd come, but he always got called away at the last minute."

"I suppose that's what we have to expect with a high-powered businessman," she said.

"Yeah, but it's still hard."

"It sure is," she agreed. "He's going to be so mad about missing this. He was really looking forward to

164

it. He wasn't allowed anywhere near when you were born."

"Have you called him?"

"I left a message at his hotel. He hadn't even arrived in England when I called."

"I wonder if he'll turn right around and come back," I said. "Maybe he'll be here for the actual birth."

"That would be nice," she said, and she grimaced. "Bad contraction," she whispered, squeezing my hand hard.

I sat with her, on and off, for most of the night. When her doctor came in to examine her, I went out to Danny. He was watching an old movie in the waiting room.

"I'm sorry to leave you alone like this," I said.

"It's okay. I always wanted to see this movie," he said.

We went to the vending machines and got hot chocolate and snacks to keep us going. I went through waves of tiredness, when my head just nodded forward and I woke as my chin jerked down. Then I would be wide awake again, the adrenaline pumping through my body.

"How long do babies normally take?" Danny asked as we attacked our third candy bar.

"I have no idea. But it seems to be getting closer. Christine's not so calm anymore and the contractions are getting stronger."

"Better her than me," Danny said.

"I agree. I think I'll adopt."

Toward dawn, they finally wheeled Christine into the delivery room. They wouldn't let me come along. I was secretly very grateful for that, since I didn't think I wanted to see what went on in there. So I went back to Danny in the waiting room, and I fell asleep with my head on his shoulder.

Suddenly, hands were shaking me. Startled, I jerked awake to see a strange woman in white standing above me.

Danny was asleep on the vinyl sofa beside me. I jumped up. "What is it? Is something wrong?" I asked.

The nurse shook her head. "You can see your mother now," she said.

That really threw me. I was still half-asleep, and I didn't even remember what my mother looked like.

"My mother?"

"Yes, she was asking for you. She's doing just fine and she has something to tell you."

I realized then that she meant Christine, of

course. I also realized that I'd never thought of her as my mother before. In fact, I'd never even thought of her as a family member. More like an intruder, usually. I hurried after the nurse. Christine was back in the pastel room, looking very tired and washed out, but peaceful.

"Hi, Justine," she said. "I thought you'd like to be the first to meet your new sister."

"My sister?" I could hardly get the words out.

She pointed to a bassinet over by the wall.

Inside the bassinet was the tiniest baby, not even as big as the doll I had practiced singing to. It had a knitted cap on its head, its eyes were shut tight, and its little fists were clenched. I looked down in wonder. Such a very tiny human being.

"Is she okay?" I asked.

Christine laughed. "From the way she cried when she was born, I'd say she was just fine."

"What's her name?"

"Your father and I thought about Alexandra. How does that sound to you? Do you think it suits her?"

I stared down at my new sister. "It seems like a big name for a small person," I said. "But we could call her Alex." I went on staring. "I like Alex. It's spunky."

I couldn't take my eyes off her. She was so tiny and so perfect. She stirred in her sleep and gave a little sigh. Then suddenly her eyes opened and she looked straight at me. Cautiously I put my hand down into the bassinet. She wrapped her little hand around my finger and held on tight.

"She's holding my finger," I said in delight.

Christine smiled. "If you're very careful, you can hold her," she said.

"Really?"

"Sure. She won't break."

I put my hand under my sister's head, the way I did with Chloe, and the other under her body. Then I lifted her up. She was much lighter than I expected, and she seemed to come flying up toward me. I sat down on the chair beside the bassinet and held her in my arms. Her eyes were still open, looking at me. This was my sister, part of my family. One day she'd grow up into a person who followed me around and got into my makeup and watched me get dressed to go on dates. And I'd fix her hair for her and buy her adorable dresses and everyone would look at us, just as I'd dreamed.

"Hi, Alexandra," I said softly. "This is your big sister, Justine. You better get used to my face, because I'm going to be around you all the time. I'm going to teach you everything I know, and if you pay attention, you're going to turn out just fine. I'm going to take you shopping and teach you to play tennis and swim and do all kinds of fun stuff. And you'll never have to worry about mean kids at school, because I'll be there for you. And I won't let them send you away to schools you don't like, and every night I'll read you a bedtime story, just like I always wanted to happen to me."

The baby's eyelids fluttered closed again and she gave a little contented sigh.

"She's asleep," I said. I looked up at Christine, and I was surprised to see that she was crying.

"She's a lucky little girl, Justine," she whispered. "With three people to adore her."

"We'll have to make sure she doesn't turn into a spoiled brat," I said with a wicked grin. "Shall I put her back?"

"No, give her to me," Christine said. "I want to hold her again. I still can't believe she's real."

I put the baby in Christine's arms. The nurse reappeared. "You'd better let Mrs. Craft get some rest now," she said.

"Rest? I want breakfast," Christine said. "It's hard work having a baby."

"And I've got to go tell Danny and call my

169

friends," I said. "They'll be so excited when I tell them I've got a baby sister and she already likes me!"

The nurse and Christine exchanged smiles. I didn't care. I was really, really happy. I had to talk to a friend. I ran down the hospital hallway, making the nurses turn around in surprise.

"Danny, guess what?" I yelled.

# About the Author

Janet Quin-Harkin has written over fifty books for teenagers, including the best-seller *Ten-Boy Summer.* She is the author of the *Friends* series, the *Heartbreak Café* series, and the *Senior Year* series. She has also written several romances.

Ms. Quin-Harkin lives with her husband in San Rafael, California. She has four children. In addition to writing books, she teaches creative writing at a nearby college.

# THE BEST OF
## THE
# ADVICE
# EXCHANGE

Boyfriend Club Central asked:

*What can you do to cheer up a friend when she's having boy trouble?*

*We got so many good responses that we're printing more of your advice:*

Be there to listen when she wants to talk about it.

- Ashley B.,
  Altoona, PA

Lend her your favorite book.

- Casandra N.,
  Cold Spring Harbor, NY

Talk to the boy she likes for her so that she won't feel embarrassed.

- Georgia M.,
Neptune City, NJ

I would invite her over, rent a movie, and eat lots of popcorn.

- Amber W.,
Orange, CA

I would tell her that she doesn't need a boyfriend because she is smart, pretty, nice, and kind.

- Tessa F., Millersburg, OH

Tell her there are lots more cute guys in the world.

- Pam H.,
Cape Coral, FL

Invite her to go shopping.

- Stephanie T., Marietta, GA

# You don't need
# —— a boyfriend to join! ——

Now you and your friends can join the real Boyfriend Club and receive a special Boyfriend Club kit filled with lots of great stuff only available to Boyfriend Club members.

- **A mini phone book for your special friends' phone numbers**
- **A cool Boyfriend Club pen**
- **A really neat pocket-sized mirror and carrying case**
- **A terrific change purse/keychain**
- **A super doorknob hanger for your bedroom door**
- **The exclusive Boyfriend Club Newsletter**
- **A special Boyfriend Club ID card**

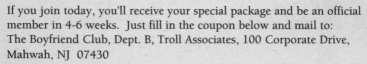

If you join today, you'll receive your special package and be an official member in 4-6 weeks. Just fill in the coupon below and mail to: The Boyfriend Club, Dept. B, Troll Associates, 100 Corporate Drive, Mahwah, NJ 07430

-------------------------------------------------------------

❏ Yes, I want to be a member of the real Boyfriend Club. I have enclosed a check or money order for $3.50 payable to The Boyfriend Club.

Name_____

Address_____

City_____State_____Zip_____

Age_____Where did you buy this book?_____

The Boyfriend Club ™

Don't miss the adventures of Ginger,
Roni, Karen, and Justine as they discover
friendship and fun in high school.

| | | |
|---|---|---|
| ____ | 0-8167-3414-3 Ginger's First Kiss #1 | $2.95 |
| ____ | 0-8167-3415-1 Roni's Dream Boy #2 | $2.95 |
| ____ | 0-8167-3416-X Karen's Perfect Match #3 | $2.95 |
| ____ | 0-8167-3417-8 Queen Justine #4 | $2.95 |
| ____ | 0-8167-3418-6 Ginger's New Crush #5 | $2.95 |
| ____ | 0-8167-3419-4 Roni's Two-Boy Trouble #6 | $2.95 |
| ____ | 0-8167-3675-8 No More Boys SPECIAL EDITION | $3.50 |
| ____ | 0-8167-3685-5 Karen's Lessons in Love #7 | $2.95 |
| ____ | 0-8167-3687-1 Roni's Sweet Fifteen #8 | $2.95 |
| ____ | 0-8167-3690-1 Justine's Baby-Sitting Nightmare #9 | $2.95 |
| ____ | 0-8167-3710-X The Boyfriend Wars SPECIAL EDITION | $3.50 |

## Available at your favorite bookstore...
## or use this form to order by mail.

Please send me the books I have checked above. I am enclosing
$_____ (please add $2.00 for shipping and handling). Send check or
money order payable to Troll Associates — no cash or C.O.D.s please — to
Troll Associates, Dept. B, 100 Corporate Drive, Mahwah, NJ 07430

Name _____

Address _____

City _____State_____Zip_____

Age_____Where did you buy this book?_____

Please allow approximately four weeks for delivery. Offer good in the U.S. only. Sorry,
mail orders are not available to residents of Canada. Prices subject to change.